FATAL PAST

TWIN OAKS SECRETS

SARAH HAMAKER

"Come unto me, ye weary, and I will give you rest."
O blessed voice of Jesus which comes to hearts
oppressed!
It tells of benediction, of pardon, grace, and peace,
Of joy that hath no ending, of love which cannot cease.

From the hymn "Come unto Me, Ye Weary," by William C.
Dix, 1867

CHAPTER

ONE

D r. Eve Davenport pushed herself to finish her 5K run strong. The day had started relatively cool, but by eleven, had heated to the upper 70s, well on the way to the 88 high predicted by her weather app. She pumped her arms as eighties pop music blared through her AirPods and accompanied her strides. The mile marker ahead on the trail indicated her stopping point and she sprinted the last fifty yards. After her stressful week, the Saturday morning run felt good. She needed to incorporate running more into her schedule, but she knew such promises would get eaten up by her long hours at her pediatrics practice, Saturday rotation at the Twin Oaks Clinic, and the monthly slot at the mobile health clinic. So she'd take today's running victory.

A few yards past the mile marker, she stopped the music on her phone, secured in an arm band, then tucked the AirPods into a pocket on her hydration belt. She drained one of the water bottles before setting off at a brisk walk toward her house another mile down the trail. One of the reasons she'd bought the small cabin was its proximity to the woods, with its miles of trails suitable for walking, biking, and running. The other had been its seclusion. Only two miles from her office in downtown Twin Oaks, the snug log house seemed miles away from civilization.

She rotated her neck, swinging her arms over head and around to ease the lingering kinks, her mind returning to the last email from her uncle, sent three days ago. The avuncular tone hadn't fooled her for an instant. Uncle Ronan Donahue, her late mother's older brother, wasn't someone she trusted, and he certainly wasn't someone who had her best interest at heart, no matter how sincere his words sounded. No, Uncle Ronan wanted something from her, and until she discovered what it was, she would not respond to his email.

"Let me go!"

The child's sobbed command jacked her pulse back into the stratosphere. Where had it come from?

Another cry of distress helped her fix the direction—the curve in the trail ahead of her—and galvanized her into action. She rounded the bend to see a man in jeans, a black t-shirt, and a baseball cap struggling to contain a squirming, screaming boy. She sized up the situation, deciding even if the man was the child's father, his actions demanded interven-tion. No way would she allow an adult to bully or harm a child in her presence.

"Hey! Leave him alone!" She made a grab for the flailing kid, but the man elbowed her in the stomach, sending her staggering back.

"Mind your own business," the man growled, adding a few choice words to emphasize his disdain. The boy took advantage of the man's inattention and slugged him in the jaw.

"You'll pay for that, you little—"

Eve kicked the man in the back of one knee with all her might. He cursed again as he fell to the ground, loosening his grip on the boy, who quickly wiggled free. Dirt streaked his face, and he hobbled, his left foot missing a shoe.

"Run!" Eve pointed in the direction she'd come from, where two trails intersected a quarter mile away. He'd at least have a chance to find help there, as many people were out in the woods enjoying the unexpected warm temperatures on this early April day.

The kid hesitated and the man lunged for him. Eve threw herself in front of the child to prevent the man from recapturing his prey. The child darted away, calling for his father. The assailant backhanded Eve across the cheek, pain exploding. If this man thought she'd crumble after a little face slap, he didn't know what she'd withstood in her teen years. She crowded his space, her movements clearly confusing him as his eyes widened. Using his surprise to her advantage, she brought her knee up as hard as she could, adding an elbow thrust into his jaw as he bent over with a yelp of pain.

"What's going on?" A tall man wearing sunglasses raced toward them.

The assailant staggered to his feet and took off running. Eve held a hand to her throbbing cheek but couldn't make her legs function enough to follow him.

The man paused in front of her. "You okay?"

"Thanks to you." She concentrated on slowing her breathing. "Did you see a boy with one shoe on the trail?"

"I'm here! This is my dad." The boy limped toward them, clearly favoring his left foot.

Relief the kid had found his father turned her bones into cooked spaghetti. "I think I need to sit down." She spied a log bench beside the trail and sank onto it.

The child joined her. "Wow, you socked the bad man good."

His admiration made her smile. "I didn't like what he did to you."

The boy's face fell. "He said to come with him, that he'd take me to find my dad and get my foot fixed. But he had mean eyes, so I said I'd wait right here. Then he tried to pick me up. That's when you came along."

"And we're very glad you did." The man thrust out a hand. "I'm Jefferson Smith."

"Eve Davenport." She shook it, glad she could attribute the shakiness of her grip to the situation and not her reaction to his name. Smith was so common, it was silly of her to assume she knew this man. Sunlight streamed through the trees, putting his face in shadows, while a close-cropped beard hid the lower half of his countenance. Despite her stern self-talk, the feeling she did know him wouldn't leave her.

"I'm Ethan," the boy said, "and I'm eight, in the second grade. We just moved to Twin Oaks last month. I stepped on something in the woods when I was looking for a ball I'd seen last week."

"Did you get a good look at the man who attacked Ethan?" Mr. Smith laid a hand on his son's shoulder, quieting the boy without embarrassing him by scolding him for his chatter.

She frowned. "It all happened so fast. He was wearing jeans, a black t-shirt, and a baseball cap pulled low. I couldn't see his eyes."

"He had a tattoo on his neck." Ethan touched the place on his own body. "It was a shamrock with some words. I couldn't read them though."

Eve drew in a sharp breath. But the man with the shamrock tattoo was after the boy, not her, and many people celebrated their Irish heritage with shamrock tattoos. It didn't mean the man was associated with her uncle.

But when her gaze collided with Mr. Smith's, who'd removed his sunglasses, the breath whooshed out of her as the brilliant blue color of his eyes registered. He might have grown a beard, but she'd recognized those eyes anywhere. By his expression, he knew who she was too. But the conversation they needed to have shouldn't take place in public.

"I'd better call 911 to report this." His voice had deepened in the intervening years since they'd been high school sweethearts.

Breaking eye contact, she lowered her head and noted the boy's sock foot. He'd said something about stepping on something. Just the distraction she needed to avoid thinking about why her former high school boyfriend was in Twin Oaks.

"May I look at your foot while your dad makes the call?"

Her soft question elicited a vigorous shake of his head no, and Ethan scooted a couple of inches away from her on the bench. His prickly response didn't faze her, as she was used to dealing with recalcitrant children. "It's okay—I'm a doctor."

"Really?" The doubt in his voice brought a brief smile to her lips.

"Guess I should have gone running in my lab coat, huh?" She crouched down in front of him. "But yes, I'm really a doctor. A pediatrician, actually, so that means—"

"You treat kids," he interrupted her, but Eve didn't mind if it gained his cooperation.

"That's right. May I?" She gestured toward the injured foot.

Ethan looked to his father for permission, the gesture telling her of the close bond between the two. Her heart ached at the thought Jefferson had married and started a family not too soon after she'd last seen him, considering Ethan's age.

Phone to his ear a step away, Jefferson nodded.

She examined the injury without removing the sock. She didn't want to contaminate the wound more. It appeared to be a puncture wound, the blood on the sock attesting to its depth. "Did you step on something sharp?"

"A nail, I think. It's still in my shoe." Ethan turned his head to the right, then left. "But I don't know where I lost it." Tears pooled in his eyes, as blue as his father's.

"No worries," she reassured the child. "I'm sure your dad can get you a new pair."

Ethan swiped at his cheeks. "Maybe."

Jefferson tucked his phone into his back jeans pocket. She rose. "I have first aid supplies at my house. It's about a half mile that way." She pointed in the correct direction. "If you want to carry him there, I can treat the wound. Is he up-to-date on his shots?"

"Yes."

"Good." As she waited for Jefferson to decide whether to go with her, she plucked at the loose t-shirt over her running bra, the stickiness of her sweat registering for the first time. Of all the scenarios she envisioned, running into Jefferson sweaty and in smelly workout clothes hadn't made the list. But it wasn't as if she needed to impress him with how wonderful her life was. He was married with a child.

"I told the dispatcher we'd meet the officer at the park's lot."

"How long did they say it would take?" She knew from experience it often took longer for a non-emergency call. An aborted kidnapping with the perpetrator long gone would be important, though, so someone would likely be coming as fast as possible.

"Less than ten minutes."

"It would be better to get Ethan's foot looked at sooner rather than later. Maybe you could ask if the police would meet you at my house? It's not far."

Her offer seemed to decide things for Jefferson. "Okay, we'll come with you." Jefferson made another call to 911, then scooped up Ethan, settling him on his back with ease. The movement emphasized his upper body strength, dredging up memories from the past that she squelched immediately.

"This way." Pasting a bright smile on her face, she pivoted. As she walked down the trail, Eve dwelled on why she'd left Boston for a sleepy town in the Shenandoah Valley of Virginia and not on a pair of fine, blue eyes and broad shoulders.

Following Eve, Jefferson carried Ethan, who chattered about how much fun he'd had playing with Mason, the puppy he'd met in the park prior to Ethan's escapade in the woods. He let his son's words wash over him while he thought about how to handle meeting Eve Donahue—no Davenport—again. She'd changed her name and fled Boston. He'd had a very good reason for leaving. What was hers? She'd seemed so close to her uncle who'd raised her after the deaths of her parents when she was little, obeying his every stricture. Most of them, anyway.

Eve veered to the right, taking an unpaved tract. The uneven ground held many potential hazards, so Jefferson shoved aside thoughts of why Eve was in Twin Oaks to concentrate on not tripping. Within a hundred yards, the trail ended in small clearing surrounding a log cabin with a wide front porch. A dark blue SUV sat in the gravel driveway.

She crossed to the front door, punching in a code on the keypad lock. Once inside, she led them toward the back of the house, which had been designed as one great room with the kitchen and dining area to the right and the living room with a massive fireplace to the left. The entire back wall consisted of floor-to-ceiling windows, which bathed the area in a golden hue from the mid-morning sunshine.

"Why don't you set Ethan on one of the counter chairs while I grab the first aid kit?" She indicated the high counter with three tall, wooden chairs tucked under the overhang. Jefferson deposited Ethan on an end chair as Eve left.

A large orange-and-white striped cat with the top of one ear missing jumped onto the countertop, his green eyes assessing the newcomers.

"Wow, look at his ear." Ethan stared at the feline. "Do you think he got into a fight?"

"Willoughby's always getting into scrapes." Eve set the first aid kit on the counter. "He adopted me when I moved here a couple of years ago." She leaned toward Ethan. "But he won't tell me how he lost part of his ear."

Ethan giggled, the sound bringing a smile to Jefferson's lips. Despite everything that had happened, his son still found plenty of reasons to laugh.

"May I have your foot?" Eve's easy demeanor soon had Ethan even more at ease as she removed his sock and examined the puncture.

Jefferson lingered behind his son to watch Eve in her doctor mode. Even as a teenager, she'd had a compassionate heart for those who were hurting.

"I'm not going to sugarcoat this. I need to clean the wound, and it's going to sting something fierce." She eyed Ethan. "But I don't think your dad will have to hold you down."

Ethan shook his head. "Nope. I can handle it."

"That's what I thought." She laid out her supplies and went to work. True to her prediction, Ethan yelped when she cleansed the area, but he didn't yank his foot away. Jefferson offered his hand, and the boy hung on tight as the doctor dabbed ointment on the wound.

She held up bright blue and olive-green rolls of self-adhesive tape. "At home, I only have two color choices, so which one do you want?"

Ethan nibbled on his lower lip, a sign of his deep concentration. "Blue."

"Good choice." She placed a gauze pad over the area, then used the blue tape to wrap the foot, securing the gauze. "Matches your eyes."

"And my dad's."

She didn't respond to Ethan's comment, her attention

focused on repacking the first aid kit. "He should stay off the foot for at least twenty-four hours. I'm going to prescribe an antibiotic as a precaution, since he acquired the wound in the woods. What pharmacy do you use?"

"I don't know. We haven't needed one."

"Twin Oaks Pharmacy on Main Street should have amoxicillin in stock. I'll need your address and phone number to write the prescription."

Jefferson gave her the information, and she wrote rapidly on a pad she'd gotten from the first aid bin, then ripped off the top sheet. "Here's the script. The pharmacy stays open on Saturdays until two, so you should have time to get it filled since it's not quite noon."

His phone buzzed with the news officers had arrived at the scene of the near-abduction. "The police are on the trail and will be at your house after they finish there."

"Sounds good." She paused. "Come see me first thing Monday morning at Twin Oaks Pediatrics on Maple—the practice opens at eight—so I can check the wound. Does he have clogs like Crocs? Those have a softer sole and should accommodate the bandage more easily."

"He does."

She held the injured foot in her hand for a moment. "I'll also write a note to excuse him from physical education and outdoor recess at school for a week."

Ethan's face fell. "No PE or recess? That's not fair."

"I know, but it's important we allow time for your wound to heal."

Jefferson thanked her.

Willoughby returned to the counter, butting his head against Ethan's arm.

"Hey, he likes me." With an ear-to-ear smile, Ethan stroked the cat's back.

"He doesn't warm up to just anybody, so you must be

special." Eve met Jefferson's gaze. "Would you mind keeping an eye on Willoughby while your dad and I talk?"

His attention never wavering from the cat, Ethan nodded.

Eve stepped over to the stone fireplace, far enough away from Ethan to avoid his eavesdropping. Jefferson decided to ask his uppermost question first. "What are you doing in Twin Oaks, and why is your name different?"

"I legally changed my name to Davenport before I entered medical school." She touched the stone mantel, running her fingers lightly over the smooth surface and avoiding his gaze. "What brings you here? Did your family relocate to Virginia after—"Her voice faltered. She cleared her throat before continuing. "After high school?"

He refused to feel sorry for the woman who'd nearly ruined his brother's life with her callous disregard, but since she'd saved Ethan from a would-be kidnapper, he wouldn't bring up the past now. "We needed a fresh start after George died." The words came out without his usual wince in remembering his fraternal twin's death. Maybe he was making progress.

Her eyes widened. "I hadn't heard. What happened?"

"Car accident." Jefferson could still hear the compassion in the emergency room doctor's voice when he'd relayed the devastating news.

"That's terrible." She raised her hand toward him but let it drop without touching him. "How long ago?"

Her brows furrowed and her nose wrinkled slightly, creating the adorable expression he'd loved to tease her about in high school. But now wasn't the time to mine those memories, so he erased them from his mind. *Until later*, a little voice whispered. He glanced over to see Ethan still playing with the cat. "Last May."

"I'm so sorry. I know you two were close." The warmth in her voice reminded him of their shared history, and he had to fight to keep a lid on his emotions. It had been nearly a year since he'd been thrust into the role of father to Ethan, and he still floundered to fulfill the position as well as George had.

"How did Ethan take George's death?"

"Not well." Her absurd question brought his annoyance—and long-simmering anger at her betrayal—back to the surface. Eve hadn't waited even a day after their breakup to hook up with his brother at their senior prom, and today she had the audacity to act as if she hadn't a clue as to who Ethan was? He frowned as he reviewed her actions with the child. She'd been courteous and friendly but gave no hint she knew the child's parentage. If that's how she wanted to play it, he'd go along—for now. Eventually, they would need to discuss it so he could keep his promise to George.

CHAPTER

TWO

Eve stepped away as Jefferson's face darkened with anger. She ducked her head as her own emotions seesawed while memories of their dating throughout their senior year of high school assailed her. An image of him breaking her heart by telling her they would no longer be a couple the day before prom filled her mind. Her fantasy about finding a way out of Boston with him had dissolved like a sugar cube in hot coffee.

"Dad!" Ethan petted Willoughby, who'd relaxed onto his side on the counter. "I'm hungry."

That was a problem she could fix, and it would give her something to do other than pepper Jefferson with questions she hadn't had the courage to ask at sixteen. She'd always wondered if it was her age or her brain that had scared him off. Jefferson and George would turn eighteen the day after high school graduation, while she had another fifteen months to go before becoming a legal adult. She'd skipped two grades in elementary school, and could have skipped another in high school, but she'd refused, wanting to spend four years with her peers before heading to college, then medical school. She'd always wanted to be a doctor.

"I can help with that." She took a mental inventory of her pantry and fridge contents, reviewing what might appeal to an eight-year-old boy. Comfort food. She pulled out a half block of gouda, butter, and milk. "How does mac and cheese sound?"

"Yay!" Ethan's eyes lit up, the expression so similar to Jefferson's when he scored during a basketball game that her breath caught in her throat. "It's my favorite."

"I don't want to put you to too much trouble, Dr. Davenport."

Jefferson's words told her he wanted to keep things formal between them, but calling her Dr. Davenport with their shared history seemed overkill. "Call me Eve, and Ethan's right—it is lunchtime. I'm fixing mac and cheese, and you both are welcome to join me."

"Please, Dad?" Ethan turned his gaze to Jefferson.

"Okay, but only if I can help with the preparations."

Eve let out a breath, as more memories flooded her, specifically of making dinner with Jefferson and George on Wednesdays at their house, the one night a week where she experienced being part of a family. "You can grate the cheese while I start the water for the noodles."

They fell into their old pattern of cooking together, almost as if they hadn't been apart for nine years. Soon Willoughby was banished from the counter, and the three of them settled down to bowls of mac and cheese, along with apple slices and glasses of fizzy water for the adults and plain water for Ethan.

"What made you decide to become a pediatrician?" Jefferson scraped his bowl for the last bite.

She put her spoon in her empty bowl. "I wanted to make a difference in the lives of kids."

"Are you?" He carried everyone's empty bowls to the sink.

"I'd like to think so." She moved toward the sink, but he waved her off.

"I've got the dishes."

Another thing she'd forgotten about Jefferson—how he always jumped in wherever he saw a need or a chore to be done.

Ethan squirmed in his chair. "Can I get down?"

"Sure, I'll help you hop to the couch so you can prop up your foot." She ruffled his hair without thinking, the texture a little stiff from dried sweat.

He nodded, and she held his hand as he slid from the tall chair. Leaning against her, he hopped on his right foot over to the couch positioned to face the fireplace with the windows to the right. After settling him on the couch, he grabbed her hand before she could return to the kitchen. "Where's your TV?"

"I don't have one."

His eyes grew large in his face. "You don't? Why not?"

"Ethan," Jefferson called from the kitchen, censure in his tone, "don't be rude."

"I wasn't, was I?" Ethan's troubled gaze bounced to her face.

"It's okay. I decided I didn't want to spoil the lovely view." She swept her hand to indicate the forest outside the windows. "Nature puts on a show every day."

"It does?" The wonder in the boy's voice warmed her heart.

"Yes. In the morning, the birds flit about, chirping to one another. Squirrels chase each other up and down the trees. Chipmunks sometimes venture onto the deck." She pointed to the rail-less deck the length of the back of the house. She hadn't wanted a railing to spoil the view, since the drop at the edges was no higher than a single stairstep. "I've even seen deer. One time"—she leaned closer to him—"I saw a mama bear and her two cubs."

"A bear! What did it look like?"

She described the black bears. By the time she'd finished, Jefferson joined them. "Shouldn't the officer be here by now?"

Eve checked her phone. It had been more than an hour since he'd called 911. "Perhaps they found clues at the scene."

"We'll give it another fifteen minutes, then I need to swing by the pharmacy to fill that prescription on our way home."

"Do we hafta leave?" Ethan whined in the classic plea to stay.

"Did you hear something?" Jefferson cocked his head as if listening hard. "I thought I might have but I'm not sure."

Ethan rolled his eyes but got his dad's meaning. "Sorry for whining. May we stay longer?"

Eve directed her attention to the glass windows. The tender exchange between father and son touched her heart, reminding her of what might have been had things turned out differently. But she firmly ignored those thoughts, not wanting to go any further down memory lane. Some things were best left in the past. A flash of black inside the tree line riming her house caught her gaze. Perhaps a bear sighting would distract them all. She stepped closer.

A rectangle-shaped object flew through the air, smashing the window and showering glass onto the floor. A piece of glass struck her cheek, drawing blood.

"Get down!" Jefferson dragged her backward to relative safety behind the loveseat on the far side of the living room. Ethan crouched there, tears streaming down his face.

First Eve had foiled a kidnapping, now someone was attacking her cabin with her, Jefferson, and Ethan inside.

Fear punched Jefferson in the gut, but he had no time to be afraid, not when Ethan and Eve were depending on him. They stayed put, Ethan trembling and Eve's face pale, until it became apparent someone was either waiting for them to move or had delivered the message via the object and had nothing left to say.

"I hear someone knocking at the front door. Must be the police." She scurried off away from the broken window before he could protest.

"Ethan, don't move." He spared a glance at his son, who nodded. "We need to be sure it's safe first."

Eve returned, a uniformed officer behind her. "This is Officer Briggs."

Now that the police had arrived, the immediate danger had passed, and Jefferson rose.

"Dad!" Ethan flung himself into his arms. "I was so scared." His little body trembled, igniting Jefferson's protective instincts as well as his anger at whoever had terrified his son.

Briggs surveyed the broken window, glass littering the hardwood floor. "Before we talk about the most recent incident, let's discuss the attempted kidnapping."

Jefferson glanced around, but Eve had disappeared. "Let's move to the kitchen to get away from the glass," Jefferson suggested.

Briggs eyed the mess and agreed.

Jefferson hoisted Ethan into his arms and carried him to one of the counter chairs. Eve came back into the room. "I locked Willoughby in my bedroom so he wouldn't get scared and try to escape out the broken window. I could use a cup of tea." She filled an electric kettle with tap water. "I have a variety of caffeinated and decaf options, including" —she waggled the kettle at Ethan—"raspberry or lemon tea."

"Raspberry tea? I've got to try that." His enthusiasm eased some of the tension from Jefferson's shoulders. Children were remarkably resilient. He wasn't fooled into thinking the boy had forgotten about the two incidents, but for now, the normalcy of drinking tea should soothe away some of his fears. If only the hot beverage would be able to ease his own troubled mind.

While the water heated, the officer walked them through the trail incident, Ethan contributing his observation of a neck tattoo in the shape of a shamrock and Eve adding her physical description of the wannabe kidnapper. She poured steaming water into mugs.

Briggs questioned them further while the tea steeped. His phone rang as Eve added a heaping spoonful of sugar to Ethan's cup.

"Excuse me a minute." Briggs walked toward the front door with his phone to his ear.

Ethan's brow furrowed as he took tiny sips of the still steaming liquid. "It does taste like raspberries!" He sipped again. "I like it."

His pronouncement triggered a chuckle from Eve, and Jefferson smiled too. One of the things he loved about Ethan was his bubbly personality. The officer returned to the kitchen.

"The forensics team didn't find any clues left behind by the kidnapper. A few people noted a man bearing the description you gave hurrying toward a pickup truck, but no one got the make or model, or could agree on the color." He shook his head. "We'll keep looking—we take attempted kidnappings very seriously. If either of you remember anything else, call us immediately. Now Dr. Davenport, why don't you walk me through what happened here?"

Eve succinctly described the events, then added her observation of the projectile. "The object was a rectangle, maybe a brick? It must have been heavy since it broke the window. I'm not sure where it landed."

"Might have been a crime of opportunity." The officer then asked for Jefferson's version of events. When he'd finished, Briggs glanced from Eve to Jefferson. "Do either of you know who might want to hurt you?"

With an effort, Jefferson resisted the urge to look at Eve. "I have no idea. We only moved to Twin Oaks in early August."

The deputy's gaze sharpened. "From where?"

"Boston."

"Why did you come here?"

Jefferson sighed, not wanting to explain about George's death and Ethan's relationship to himself. "After my brother died, Ethan was having trouble in school. Since I can work anywhere, we decided to move farther south."

"What kind of trouble?"

Briggs directed his question at Jefferson, but Ethan piped up. "Some kids were bullying me, and the teacher wouldn't do anything about it because one of the kids was the principal's daughter."

"That must have been tough." Eve squeezed Ethan's hand. "I hope you're not finding any bullies in your second-grade class here."

"Nope. Everyone's been great." He slurped his tea. "Can we leave soon? I wanna watch *Teen Titans*."

"In a couple of minutes." Jefferson returned his attention to the officer, who had moved on to asking Eve if she knew of any personal enemies.

She shook her head. "No one comes to mind. I moved to Twin Oaks two years ago from Baltimore after completing my pediatrics residency training at Johns Hopkins."

"You don't look old enough to be a doctor." The young policeman flushed. "I'm sorry, ma'am. I didn't mean—"

"It's okay." She smiled at the blushing man. "I finished high school at sixteen, then did my undergraduate work in two and a half years instead of four, so..." She shrugged, discounting her intelligence as a negligible thing instead of an integral part of what made her such a warm, compassionate woman.

You left out gorgeous. Jefferson ignored the thought as Briggs completed his interview.

"Did you see where the projectile landed?"

Eve shook her head. "It all happened so fast, but maybe by the fireplace?"

Jefferson said he hadn't seen the object land either and, leaving Ethan to finish his tea at the counter, they entered the living room to search for the stone or brick. Eve spotted the brick in the fireplace, where it likely had bounced after impact with the floor. The officer tracked several indentations on the wood planks marking its path after shattering the glass.

He took several photos of the brick in the fireplace before snapping on gloves and removing it.

"Shouldn't you leave it for the crime scene techs?" Eve voiced the question Jefferson had been about to ask.

Briggs shook his head. "In cases like this, where nothing was stolen and the intruder didn't enter the house, we collect evidence at the scene. We've all been trained in evidentiary recovery. If we think it needs a more thorough going over, we'll get the tech guys in." He hefted the brick as if testing its weight. "Do you have any newspaper I could rest this on?"

Eve reached into the box beside the fireplace and spread several sheets of newspaper on the floor. Briggs laid the brick on it, giving Jefferson his first clear view of the object.

Painted on the upper facing flat side were the words: *Your days are numbered.*

THREE

Eve sucked in a breath as the words walloped her emotions. The blatant threat shocked her but was the message directed at her or Ethan, given the kidnapping attempt?

"Look," Ethan said, pointing to the side of the brick, "there's a shamrock."

This time, Eve couldn't contain the gasp as she found the trio of green leaves. She bent for a closer look. No words adorned it like Ethan had seen on the man's neck tattoo, but the fact a shamrock was included in the message disturbed her.

"You okay?" Jefferson touched her arm while Briggs snapped photos of the brick from all angles.

"No." She couldn't look away from the brick, the implications of the symbol of Ireland, coupled with the message, creating a corresponding rock in her stomach. "But we need to talk."

Briggs put away his camera. "I'll take this to the lab to check for fingerprints, then do a perimeter sweep to see if I can find where the perp stood to toss the object into your house."

"Thank you." If her uncle was behind the attack, there would be nothing to find. He only hired the best of the best to do his dirty work. "Is it okay to clean up the glass and board up the window?"

"That's fine. Do you need a recommendation to help with the window?"

Before she could accept the offer, Jefferson jumped in. "I can cut a board to fit and install it this afternoon."

"Then I'll get that evidence bag." Briggs left the room.

"You don't have to do that," she began but Jefferson waved her off.

"I'm a carpenter, and I have large sheets of plywood at my shop. Won't take me very long."

"But we were supposed to make pizza and watch a movie later today." Ethan's protest ended with a pout.

Eve found the little boy's facial expression adorable but smothered her smile as Jefferson addressed his son.

"This won't take long."

"That's what you always say, and it always takes forever." Ethan dragged out the last word, his displeasure growing by the seconds.

Time to step in. "I have an idea." She waited until she had their attention. "Your dad measures the window now, then takes you home after picking up the antibiotic. I'll clean up this mess and come to your house to get started on the pizza while your dad comes to my house to board the window." When neither one of them said anything, she added, "I have a secret ingredient that makes my pizza the best you'll ever taste."

Ethan shrugged, clearly not sold on her ability to produce an edible result, despite having gobbled up her mac and cheese. "I suppose."

Jefferson squeezed the boy's shoulder. "If Dr. Davenport comes over to handle pizza duty, I'll be back in time to eat with you and watch the movie."

"Okay." Ethan didn't sound like it was okay, but Jefferson acted as if the child had enthusiastically agreed. "But can I still watch *Teen Titans* now on your phone?"

"One episode, since we're watching *Puss in Boots* later."

The boy huffed but quieted. Eve directed Jefferson to her junk drawer where she kept a tape measure, then asked for the prescription back so she could enter his address into her phone. While Jefferson stepped over to the broken window, she sat beside Ethan on the loveseat. "Is your foot hurting?"

Tears welled in Ethan's eyes, some spilling onto his cheeks. "Yeah."

"I'll get you some pain reliever." Eve hurried from the room to her locked medicine cabinet in the hall linen closet. She extracted the correct dosage of children's ibuprofen chewable tablets and relocked the cabinet before returning to Ethan. "Here you go. You chew them up."

"Cool. Dad only gives me the liquid kind." He popped the tablets in his mouth. "I hate the way it tastes."

"Medicine doesn't always taste like ice cream." She returned to her seat beside him.

"Can you really make pizza as good as my dad's?"

His comment brought back a vivid memory of George and Jefferson competing for title of best pizza maker in the Smith family. She'd been folded into their family pizza competitions and won a time or two. "I'm not too shabby."

"Good." The change in topic had done little to ease whatever was worrying the small boy, if his woebegone expression was any indication of his feelings.

"Anything else wrong?"

"I'm scared."

"It's been a scary day." She patted his shoulder.

He leaned into her, his body snuggling closer. "I'm afraid I'll have the bad dreams again, like I had after my first dad died."

His words tangled in her brain. First dad? Her gaze

whipped to Jefferson, still measuring the broken window. She had to ask the question burning her tongue, even though she suspected the answer. "Who was your first dad?"

The boy sniffled, wiping his wet cheeks with the back of his hand. "George, my second dad's twin."

"I see." She didn't, but the kid wouldn't have answers to the questions now pummeling her mind. Not wanting to think about the implications of Ethan being George's child, not Jefferson's, she rose.

Leaning against the wall out of sight of Ethan and Jefferson, she drew in a shuddering breath to calm her roiling emotions. George had had a child, one who would have been the exact age of her and George's baby if the infant hadn't died during delivery.

Or had that been another lie her uncle had told her?

JEFFERSON DIRECTED EVE TO HOLD HER END OF THE GLASS IN place while he checked the fit. Perfect. It had been four days since someone had tossed a brick through the floor-to-ceiling window. The local glass maker had a piece large enough for the replacement in stock, saving Eve weeks of having to look at the ugly plywood he'd installed. On Saturday, Eve had made the pizza as promised but left as soon as he'd returned home. While he hadn't expected they would fall into their old familiarity from high school, her abrupt departure signaled she wasn't ready to start a tentative new friendship. That didn't bode well for him to fulfill the promise he'd made to George, especially when she'd barely spoken to him since he'd arrived to install the glass.

He certainly wasn't going to push to have the conversation his brother had begged him to have with Eve, so he didn't try to breach the *No Trespassing* barriers she'd placed around herself. On the deck, he finished securing the glass, stepping back to ensure it fit snugly all around the frame. He waved to Eve on the inside, gesturing he'd come around to check the interior fit as well. She nodded her understanding.

In the living room, he doublechecked the pane of glass. "There, good as new."

She surveyed the window. "Thank you. I appreciate the help."

Overlooking the stiffness in her words, he squatted to repack his toolkit. "I'm happy to help."

"How's Ethan's foot?"

He locked the metal box and stood. "On the mend. He seems to have forgotten all about the attempted kidnapping and vandalism here, probably because he was so excited about today's class trip to the nature center a few miles outside of town."

That brought a brief smile to her lips. "Ah, the resilience of the young."

"I know what you mean. He was hopping about the place on one foot Sunday morning, and I needed two cups of coffee to wake up enough to get to the worship service on time."

Her eyebrows rose. "You attend church?"

He managed not to wince at the surprise in her voice. "Yeah, quite a change from our teenage years when we wouldn't have darkened the doors of a church."

A haunted look flashed across her features before she schooled her face into blank politeness. "What made you change your mind?"

"Not what, who—George." Jefferson swallowed the lump the size of a brick in his throat at the remembrance of his brother's words a few weeks before he died. Her question also gave him the opening he needed to talk about George's last request, since it included her. "George talked a lot about God and how everything works out for our good and his glory. I didn't understand how he could say such things, given what he'd witnessed as a cop. George left me a letter along with his will, asking me to take Ethan to church, so I did." He tried to find the right words to tell Eve how he'd realized how much he needed God, especially as he grieved the loss of his twin.

"I'm glad to hear about George's faith." She broke eye contact. "I had a professor in college who talked to me about God at a time when I needed to believe in something bigger than myself. I go to Twin Oaks Community's early service when I'm not working at the migrant clinic during the apple picking season."

That explained why he hadn't run into her, as he and Ethan usually went to the mid-morning service at the same church. His phone rang, intruding on the moment. He glanced at the screen, prepared to ignore it but saw the number was from Twin Oaks Elementary. "It's the school, so I'd better take it."

She nodded and went into the kitchen as he answered the call. "Hello?"

"Mr. Smith? It's Assistant Principal Laney Blair."

"What can I do for you, Ms. Blair?" Jefferson tightened his grip on the phone. He'd only spoke to the assistant principal once when Ethan had spit at another child during a dispute over a seat in the lunchroom.

"I'm afraid there's been an incident."

"What kind of incident?" Her cryptic words made him uneasy, as if sensing something more was wrong than a spat between second graders.

"We're still sorting out the details."

He wasn't reassured by her words. "Please tell me what happened. Where's Ethan?"

Eve returned to his side, her eyes wide as she listened to his side of the conversation.

"He and the other children were having some free time at the nature center, and well, you know how rowdy kids that age can be."

"Is Ethan okay?" His impatience with the woman's round-about way of telling him what happened to his son changed his tone to a growl.

"I'm sorry, Mr. Smith." The assistant principal drew in a breath. "The incident has shaken us all very badly. Bear with me, please."

While she paused, Jefferson put the phone on speaker so Eve could hear too. He wasn't sure why he wanted her to, but he figured she deserved to know.

"The teacher had the children line up to board the bus for school, but Ethan wasn't with them." Ms. Blair's voice hitched. "He's missing."

FOUR

E ve's heart kicked into high gear at the woman's words. Although she'd only known Ethan a short time, the little guy had wormed his way into her affections.

"What do you mean missing?" Jefferson leaned over the phone, the panic in his voice echoing her own thumping heart.

"We can't find him. The teacher looked around and asked the other children if anyone had seen him. Then she alerted the staff, who scoured the buildings and wooded pathways, but he's not there."

"How long has my son been missing?" The controlled anger in his voice reminded Eve how protective Jefferson could be.

She laid a hand on his forearm, a gesture she'd done often to calm him down when they were teenage sweethearts. He flinched at her touch, and she removed her hand as fast as if she'd been scalded. At least his attention was still directed at the phone and not at her flaming face, as if her embarrassment mattered with Ethan missing.

"Ninety minutes or so," the woman replied. "We've called

the police, as the center doesn't have the manpower to search the woods."

"I'm on my way." He disconnected the call, shoving the phone into his pocket. "I've got to go."

"I'm coming with you." She'd intended to work from home the rest of the day to catch up on paperwork, but that could wait. She wanted, no needed, to be part of the search for Ethan. When he hesitated, she added, "I know a shortcut to get to the center. It'll be faster than driving through town."

At his nod, she snatched her keys and headed to the door, Jefferson at her heels, glad he hadn't fussed about her driving. Once on the road, she let the silence build between them during the short ride to the Twin Oaks Nature Center. Thoughts around what Ethan had let slip about George being his first dad swirled in her mind faster and faster like a tornado. The possibility her uncle had lied to her, had let her believe all these years her baby had died, wouldn't leave her thoughts. But she lacked the courage to ask Jefferson the truth because her heart couldn't bear to hear Ethan wasn't her son. It would be like losing her child all over again, and she barely survived the loss the first time.

No, she would bide her time and hope that she could figure out who Ethan's mother was on her own. Now most definitely wasn't the time to uncork that particular question, not with the child in question missing.

She swung the SUV into the parking lot of the center, wedging it between two police cruisers. Jefferson opened his door the moment she'd put the car in Park, and she grabbed her phone and dashed after him, pushing her way through a group of children and adults gathered on the sidewalk near the front entrance.

"I'm Jefferson Smith, Ethan's dad," Jefferson announced to a trio of uniformed police officers talking to a flustered young woman wearing a lanyard.

"Mr. Smith, I'm Officer Delaney with the Twin Oaks Police Department. We're organizing a search of the grounds."

Eve edged closer to Jefferson, not wanting to miss a word.

"I'm so sorry, Mr. Smith." The young woman sniffled, her cheeks wet with tears. "Ethan's never wandered off by himself before. He's always such a good listener in class."

"Ms. Glennings, did any of the children see where Ethan might have gone?" Jefferson spoke in an even tone.

Eve admired his self-restraint. In her profession, she often saw parents unable to control their emotions when worrying about their child.

"No." She swiped at her face with the back of one hand. "I asked and no one remembers seeing him after we finished the loop with the tour guide. I gave the children fifteen minutes of free time to play on the grounds, but I reminded them the paths through the woods were off limits."

Eve glanced at the kids milling about with several of the center's staff keeping an eye on them. One little girl stood apart from the group. She dragged the toe of her sneaker through the dirt over and over again, making a pattern only she could see. Something about the way she was separated from the rest of the children tugged at Eve's heart. She remembered that feeling of aloneness in a crowd of her peers. Because she skipped several grades, the older children never really accepted her into their groups, and she rarely had the chance to spend time with kids her own age.

She walked over to the second grader. "Hi, I'm Dr. Eve."

The little girl didn't look at Eve, just continued drawing a circle in the dirt with the toe of her sneaker.

"Do you mind if I watch you draw?"

The girl shrugged, her attention on the ground.

Eve wasn't deterred by the lack of verbal response. At her practice, she could coax even the most reluctant child into speech. "Do you know Ethan?"

A quick nod, followed by a lightning-fast glance in Eve's

direction. They were making progress. Time to get specific. "Ethan's missing."

"He's not missing."

Eve picked up a stick and drew a square a few inches from the girl's expanding circle. "He's not?"

The girl shook her head, sending her ponytail swinging. "You can't be missing if you're with someone, can you?"

Eve considered the question. "I suppose not." She let several seconds pass before asking, "Who is with Ethan?"

The girl shrugged. "I don't know."

"Was it a man?"

"Yes."

Eve flashed back to the scene on the path near her house where she'd first met Ethan. "Did Ethan want to go with the man?"

That question seemed to puzzle the girl, who wrinkled her nose as if thinking. "I'm not sure. At first, no, but then the man said something, and Ethan went with him."

Eve tried to temper her rising excitement. "Did you hear what the man said?"

"Nope, too far away." The girl kicked a rock, sending up a small cloud of dust into Eve's face.

Coughing, she waited until the dust settled before asking another question. "Where did this happen?"

The girl pointed toward the woods. "Ethan's shoe had come untied, so he stopped to tie it. But he's not very fast on account of his hurt foot, so the others left him behind."

Eve pictured what had happened. Ethan pausing to tighten his shoelace, the other children continuing to walk back to the center. "Why didn't an adult wait with him?"

The girl shrugged. "Don't know. I wanted to pick one of the wildflowers." She clapped a hand over her mouth, her eyes huge. "We weren't supposed to."

Eve leaned closer. "I won't tell." She crossed her heart to prove her point.

The girl must have believed her because she went on. "So I guess I was the only one who saw the man step out of the woods near Ethan."

Eve questioned the girl a little more but gained no new insights. "Did you tell Ms. Glennings what you saw?"

At the mention of the teacher's name, the child's eyes filled with tears. "I did, but she said to stop telling lies."

Anger ignited inside Eve at hearing the teacher had discounted a lead to what might have happened to Ethan. "Why would she say that?"

The girl stamped her foot. "Because Nataly and Francesca keep telling Ms. Glennings about all the lies I've said, only I haven't. I don't. They're the liars. They do things, then blame me. And now she thinks I lie all the time." She broke into sobs, her small shoulders shaking.

Eve gathered her in her arms, soothing the child as her mind raced with the implications of what she'd learned.

Ethan hadn't wandered off.

Someone had kidnapped him.

Jefferson scrubbed a hand over his beard in an attempt to keep from snapping at everyone to stop talking and look for his son. But he knew the police needed to be systematic in their search or they might miss a vital clue as to Ethan's whereabouts. To distract himself while he waited, he looked for Eve.

The doctor crouched next to a girl drawing in the dirt with her sneaker away from the other children. Her natural rapport with kids probably made her an excellent pediatrician, but he couldn't help but contrast that with ignoring her own son. Not once had she contacted George over the eight years of Ethan's life. Not once had she attempted to see her child. And not once since they'd met had she even acted like she knew Ethan was her son.

Jefferson had come to Twin Oaks to rebuild his life with Ethan, needing a fresh start without constant reminders of his brother. The small town, with its central location in the middle of the Shenandoah Valley, gave him accessibility to larger cities for his handmade wooden furniture designs while providing a quieter life for him and Ethan. His conscience smarted over his delay in fulfilling the wish George had expressed in his letter to find Eve and let her be part of Ethan's life. But Jefferson had put that search into the "one day" category, not having the mental energy required to face his high school sweetheart, not with George's passing still so fresh.

Their reconnecting after all these years reminded him of a line from *Casablanca*, Eve's all-time favorite movie: "Of all the gin joints in all the towns in all the world, she walks into mine." Of all the towns in all the world, he had to move to the one where she lived. The object of his musings rose and came toward him with the little girl's hand tucked into her own, and he pasted what he hoped would be a welcoming expression on his face.

"Jefferson, Belinda says she saw Ethan leave with a man."

"What?" Jefferson tempered his response as Belinda's eyes widened. He listened as Eve recounted what Belinda had told her.

"Belinda, what have you been telling Mr. Smith?" Ms. Glennings joined them, her frown deepening as Eve relayed the information about the man who had taken Ethan. "I'm so sorry, but Belinda lies to get attention."

"I'm not lying!" Belinda crossed her arms as tears sprang to her eyes. "I saw the man talking to Ethan, then they left together."

"Stop it!" The teacher's voice rose, drawing the attention

of nearby police officers. "You need to tell the truth. There was no man, was there?"

"There was! He was tall and had on a grey sweatshirt with the hood up." Belinda's body shook, and Eve slipped an arm around the girl's shoulders.

"What's this about a man?" Officer Delaney interjected before Ms. Glennings could berate the child more.

"Belinda says she saw a man talking to Ethan in the woods, and that Ethan walked off with the man," Jefferson said, fear wrapping its familiar arm around his neck and squeezing tight. He sucked in air like a man drowning, refusing to give into the paralyzing emotion. He couldn't lose Ethan. It would be like losing George all over again, and he'd barely survived that.

"You can't trust a word she says," Ms. Glennings said.

"Thank you, Ms. Glennings, but I'll hear what Belinda has to say." Officer Delaney addressed the girl. "Would you tell me what you saw?"

Belinda sniffed, then nodded. As she told about Ethan stopping to tie his shoe and a man stepping out of the woods, Jefferson inwardly seethed at the teacher's arbitrary decision to ignore the little girl's story simply because she'd labeled Belinda a liar. When she finished, Officer Delaney asked a few more clarifying questions, then stepped away to confer with the gathering officers and volunteers for the search. Even though Belinda's story pointed to a kidnapping, the officer explained they would continue with their planned search of the woods surrounding the center as soon as the tracking dogs arrived onsite. In addition, an Amber alert had been issued.

Jefferson calculated how many hours of daylight were left on the breezy April day. Probably close to three, but the woods would limit the amount of sunlight with some of the trees in full bloom already, given the warmer-than-usual spring. Would it be enough to find clues as to where the man had taken Ethan?

Ms. Glennings had cornered Belinda, talking low and fast to the girl. Ethan hadn't commented much about his teacher, but Jefferson didn't like what he'd seen thus far in the young woman. Anyone who berated a child in public didn't have his respect, much less a person in authority like a teacher. He also fumed about Ms. Glennings' decision to quash Belinda's story because she doubted the veracity of the tale.

Eve clearly agreed the teacher had overstepped her authority, if her stiff posture and frown were any indication. She inserted herself into the conversation between the teacher and student. The teacher reared back, her nostrils flaring and her eyebrows rising at whatever Eve had said.

"She's sending everyone on a wild goose chase, mark my words." Ms. Glennings crossed her arms across her chest. "She's always telling tall tales."

"No, I'm not," Belinda protested. "That's Nataly and Francesca—they're the ones who don't tell the truth."

"This isn't helpful, Ms. Glennings." Eve's firm voice—and pointed look—brought an end to the conversation.

Ms. Glennings opened her mouth, then snapped it closed and left without voicing any additional opinions.

Eve laid her hand on the girl's shoulder. "You did a great job in describing the man."

Belinda straightened under Eve's praise. "Dr. Eve, I did remember one more thing."

"What was that?"

"He had one of those Irish green flowers on his ankle. I forget what it's called."

"A shamrock?"

"Yes, that's it. A small, green shamrock. I saw it because his pants didn't go all the way down to his shoes. I don't think he was wearing socks, because I didn't see any. Why would someone not wear socks?"

"I don't know." Eve nodded toward the playground, where Ms. Glennings was herding the children toward a school bus. "I think your class is heading out. Thanks again for your help."

"I hope you find Ethan. He's nice." With a wave, Belinda scampered off toward the bus.

Jefferson didn't think the girl was lying, but then again, his sole experience with kids was with Ethan. While he didn't want to believe someone had kidnapped his son, he wouldn't discount the possibility out of hand.

Eve stepped closer to him, sending the subtle scent of rosemary he'd always associated with her into his sphere. "This can't be a coincidence."

"What can't?"

"These shamrocks. First the man who tried to take Ethan on the path near the park had one on his neck. Then the brick through my window had shamrock painted on the side, now this one on the kidnapper's ankle."

As she ticked off the shamrock sightings, Jefferson's gut clenched. George had been doodling the symbol on scraps of paper in the weeks before he'd died. Jefferson had found the distinctive three leaves on bills, grocery lists, and in the margins of George's favorite cookbook. "What are you saying?"

Her brown eyes darkened with worry. "I think my uncle might be behind these attacks."

FIVE

"What?" Jefferson voiced the question louder than he'd intended. Several officers organizing the growing crowd of volunteers for the search glanced his way. He lowered his tone, leaning closer to Eve. "Why would your uncle want to kidnap Ethan?"

She dropped her gaze, her shoulders rounding. "He's a dangerous man involved in…things."

"What things?" His tone could have been less strident, but worry over his missing son made him irritable. He mentally reviewed what he knew about Ronan Donahue, a tough man who'd kept a strict eye on his niece. The self-made man had run several successful businesses, including a construction company and a regional convenience store chain. Donahue had his fingers in a lot of pies, but he gave back hundreds of thousands of dollars every year to local charities and employed half the town of Southborough outside of Boston in his various businesses.

"I don't know for sure, but I think he might be a member of the Irish mob."

The Irish mob. Now he'd heard everything. Jefferson blew out a breath. Donahue had been quite candid when he'd appeared at the Smith home with the newborn Ethan in a car seat carrier. *Eve refuses to have anything to do with the baby. She said her dream of becoming a doctor came first. She never wants to hear from you or get any updates on the baby ever. I'm sorry. She probably told you some sob story about how she was treated badly by me over the years. I did my best to raise her after her parents died, but sometimes…* He'd left the rest unspoken, his pain over Eve's actions obvious from his teary eyes. His parents had appeared as shocked as Jefferson and George had been, since Eve had been welcomed in their home prior to the pregnancy. But Eve had ignored their phone calls and letters for months, so Donahue's words rang true. Now hearing Eve say her uncle might be connected with the Irish mob seemed outlandish.

"You don't believe me." Eve's flat tone broke into his thoughts.

Jefferson shrugged, not wanting to rehash the past, not when Ethan was missing. He longed to join the searchers, who now fanned out from the center in all directions in an orderly manner, but Officer Delaney had stressed the importance of his staying put to be available to answer any additional questions. "It's doesn't jive with your uncle's public persona."

"No, it doesn't, but I can tell you from personal experience, he wasn't a man to be crossed." A shadow darkened the spark in her eyes.

"Mr. Smith!" Officer Delaney jogged toward them, his face less grim than it had been earlier. "A dog walker just reported finding Ethan on a path about a mile and a half from here."

Elation pumped through Jefferson. "Is he okay?" *Please let Ethan be all right!*

"He's more frightened than hurt, according to Mr. Myers, the dog's owner. I have officers heading there now." Officer Delaney led the way to a police cruiser. "The path backs up to a neighborhood of single-family homes, so it will take us a few minutes to drive there from here."

"Does that path connect to the ones around the nature center?"

"No, there's a creek that runs alongside the neighborhood pathway." Officer Delaney reached his cruiser and chirped open the doors. "We'll find out more from Ethan once we arrive."

"Should I come with you in case Ethan needs medical treatment?" Eve's question surprised Jefferson, as he hadn't noticed her following him to the vehicle.

"Good idea, Dr. Davenport," the policeman answered before Jefferson could.

Jefferson climbed in the backseat, Eve buckling in beside him. During the short ride to the neighborhood, he alternated between expressing silent thanks to God for Ethan's safe recovery and puzzlement as to why his son had become a target of kidnappers. Eve's assertion her uncle was behind it didn't make any sense to Jefferson. If Donahue had wanted to harm Ethan, he could have done so in the years when the two families lived close by in the Boston area.

Her pointing the blame to Donahue shored up the man's tale that she had been a wild teenager, bent on having her own way. While Jefferson hadn't seen that side of her when they were together, Eve's hooking up with his brother at prom less than twenty-four hours after they'd broken up proved Donahue's story. Seeing her again had ignited all of his anger and frustration over her treatment of Ethan—and himself and George.

His brother's confession several years ago that he had tricked Eve into consuming alcohol laced with Ecstasy during the after-prom party had assuaged some of his hurt feelings over Eve's fast defection from himself to his brother. He could even understand how their sexual encounter happened so easily that night. But he couldn't forgive her for how she'd callously dumped Ethan on George through her uncle and refused to talk about it, despite his and George's numerous attempts through in-person visits, texts, phone calls, and emails. George had even mailed a couple of letters to her but nothing generated a response.

The cruiser turned into a cul-de-sac and parked perpendicular to the curb in the circle. Jefferson shoved all thoughts of Eve and their shared past back into his heart vault. Time to focus on Ethan. He exited the vehicle as soon as Officer Delaney disengaged the locks and spotted his son sitting on a bench near a paved path. A man holding the leash of a yellow lab stood nearby talking with a policewoman.

"Dad!" Ethan launched himself at Jefferson, who caught him in a hug. "I was so scared."

"It's okay, buddy. I've got you." Jefferson held his son tight. Eve and Officer Delaney approached, and he loosened his hold slightly to talk to Ethan. "Dr. Davenport's here, so why doesn't she take a quick look at you to make sure you're okay."

"I'm fine." Ethan jutted out his lower lip. "I don't want a doctor."

Jefferson squeezed Ethan. "I know."

"It won't take long, I promise." Eve waited while Ethan seemed to consider.

Then he rubbed a fist in his eye, a sure sign his son was tired. "I suppose."

Jefferson placed the boy on the ground. Eve held out her hand and Ethan slipped his into hers. The pair walked back to the bench while the dog walker and other officer came to where Jefferson and Officer Delaney stood.

"Mr. Smith, this is David Myers, who found Ethan," said the female police officer.

"I wouldn't say I found him," Mr. Myers protested. "It would be more accurate to say Ethan found me and Milo."

The dog woofed at hearing its name, breaking some of the tension. "May I pet Milo?"

"Of course." Mr. Myers loosened his grip on the lead, allowing Milo to come closer to Jefferson, who scratched the dog behind his ears. Several more police vehicles entered the cul-de-sac and parked.

"What happened?" Jefferson glanced at the bench where Eve sat beside Ethan, an open first aid kit an officer must have given her on her lap. He'd noticed some lacerations on Ethan's face and arms, probably from branches or bushes during his trek through the woods.

"Hold that thought, please." Delaney waved toward a tall woman in slacks and a blazer. The woman came over to their group.

"Mr. Smith, this is Detective Janice Cunningham with the Twin Oaks City Police Department," Delaney said. "She'll be the lead investigator on your son's kidnapping."

"I'm glad your son has been recovered without apparent harm," the detective said.

"Dr. Davenport is examining him to make sure he's okay physically," Delaney interjected.

Jefferson nodded, unable to speak around the lump in his throat as the thought he could have lost his son assailed him once again.

Delaney introduced the dog walker, then Detective Cunningham took over the questioning. "Mr. Myers, please tell me how you encountered Ethan."

"We were walking on the trail," he pointed to the asphalt path, "and were about a half mile into the woods when I heard yelling. Milo began barking, then Ethan burst out of the woods on the other side of the creek. A man was chasing him, but when he saw me, he turned and ran back into the woods. I called to Ethan to tell him to cross a little farther down where the water's shallower and there are some stones to walk on. Milo and I went to the place, keeping Ethan company on the other side, and he crossed safely. Then he told me to call the police because the man I saw had grabbed him from the nature center."

The detective asked a few more questions, but the dog walker couldn't shed any more light on the man who had taken Ethan. Myers's description was vague enough to be useless, and he'd been too far away to notice any ankle tattoos. Frustration threatened to overwhelm Jefferson, but Cunningham appeared to take the incident very seriously, and he had no doubt she would conduct a thorough investigation. She verified they had Mr. Myers' contact info before letting the man leave.

"Mr. Smith, we'd like to talk with Ethan now, if that's okay with you."

"Of course." Jefferson wanted nothing more than to gather his son in his arms and barricade themselves in their three-bedroom home, but he knew Ethan had to share what happened in order for the police to have all the pertinent details to catch the culprit.

Eve and Ethan returned from the bench, the boy chattering away as they walked hand and hand toward them. Jefferson's heart stuttered at how alike they were—Ethan's hair nearly an identical shade to Eve's shoulder-length chestnut locks. But no matter how touching the scene was, Jefferson reminded himself of how Eve gave Ethan up without a backward glance. His heart might still find her even more attractive as a woman of twenty-five than he had a girl of sixteen, but his mind blared warnings to stay away.

～

EVE REVIEWED THE TEST RESULTS, THEN SIGHED. MRS. Singletary would not be pleased to hear her son did not have strep. If Eve could give the diagnosis she wanted to, she would tell Mrs. Singeltary that Terrance was a healthy ten-year-old with a very worried mother. Every sniffle or cough brought them into the office with a list of possible conditions Mrs. Singletary had researched on "Dr. Google."

But each patient deserved to be treated with respect, and that extended to the accompanying parent. She braced herself for pushback when she would not prescribe an antibiotic for the viral sore throat Terrance had.

"Mrs. Singletary poked her head out of exam room two again." Cynthia Gilbert, one of the nurses at Twin Oaks Pediatrics, grimaced as she entered the small lab. She nodded at the paper in Eve's hand. "Let me guess—negative for strep."

"As well as negative for flu, RSV, and Covid. The kid has a virus and will be fine by tomorrow." Eve bottled up another sigh. She tried to keep a professional demeanor even out of earshot of her patients.

Cynthia shuddered. "Better you than me telling that she-bear her little cub has to suffer through the symptoms without an antibiotic."

Eve smothered a smile behind the paper. Cynthia's asides could be very funny, but sometimes they bordered on inappropriate, so Eve had learned not to encourage the nurse. "I'd better go deliver the good news."

The nurse guffawed. "She won't see it like that."

Eve left without addressing the comment, heading toward exam room two. Before she could open it, Lily Turnbolt, office manager and Eve's best friend, hailed her.

"Eve, the claim for Ethan Smith was rejected again by his insurance company. This time, I called and they said the policy lapsed last year."

"Did you let Mr. Smith know?"

"I've left two voicemails over the past three days, but he hasn't returned my calls."

Usually Lily handled insurance issues without bothering Eve about it, but ever since Eve had let it slip she'd known

Jefferson in high school, Lily had been not-so-subtly hinting Eve should pursue the single dad. "Okay, I'm not sure—"

"Normally, I'd wait a little longer, but we have that auditor coming at the end of the month, so I've been trying to make sure our accounts are up-to-date."

This time, Eve let the sigh escape. "I'll call him once I've finished with my patients. I was planning on staying late to catch up on paperwork anyway."

"Thanks." A ringing phone drew Lily's attention. "I'd better get that. I can't wait for Susan to come back from her honeymoon next week and man the front desk again."

Eve dictated a memo to call Jefferson into her phone notes app, then pushed open the door to greet an agitated Mrs. Singletary and a bored Terrance. The rest of the afternoon flew by with minor ailments and checkups. Eve always thanked God when a day only brought run-of-the-mill appointments. Some doctors might find that boring, but not her. The less excitement at the practice, the better. At least with a full day of appointments, she had little time to think about Jefferson and Ethan.

It had been three days since the attempted kidnapping, and she hadn't heard a peep from Jefferson with any updates on the case. Ethan had described how the man had asked for help finding a lost puppy who had run off into the woods, and Ethan had agreed. But once away from the path, the man had grabbed his arm and started dragging him through the woods. Ethan had resisted but hadn't been able to get away until the man had tripped on a rock and let go. Ethan had run as fast as he could and had found the man with the dog just as the kidnapper had spotted Ethan. Ethan hadn't noticed any tattoos or any other details about the kidnapper's appearance. His description had been of an ordinary man with a full beard and sunglasses, and Ethan had been adamant he wasn't the man from the earlier attempt. Other than some scratches from bushes or trees, Ethan appeared to have weathered the incident fine. Eve hoped Jefferson had taken her advice and lined up a therapist who specialized in trauma to speak with Ethan.

Eve shook her head as if to clear away thoughts of Jefferson and Ethan. She needed to focus on her work, or she'd have to come in Saturday afternoon to finish after her shift at the clinic. Over the next couple of hours, she updated her case notes, then followed up on a newborn baby who had been running a fever and a fifth-grader who had broken his leg climbing the lattice wall in his mother's rose garden in an attempt to mimic spiderman. After stretching her arms over her head, she executed a few chair yoga poses to loosen her stiff muscles.

Her desk and cell phones caught her eye with each stretch, mocking her attempt to avoid making the call to Jefferson. *Stop procrastinating. You have a legitimate reason to call.* But her self-talk did little to calm the butterflies fluttering in her stomach. Once she'd deemed no physical harm had come to Ethan and returned him to his father, Jefferson hadn't given her a chance to further explain why she thought her uncle might be behind the attacks on Ethan. Part of her couldn't fault Jefferson for not believing her because Ronan Donahue had cultivated a public persona very different from the face he showed at home. Both her uncle and his wife Lorraine dropped their masks when no one but close family was around, and Eve's childhood had been filled with belittling comments and cruel punishments. If she didn't bring home perfect test scores, she would be fed only bread and water for a week. If she asked questions about her own parents, who had died in a car accident when Eve was a toddler, she was locked in her room at night.

Eve had never shared those stories with Jefferson, not even when they'd become a steady couple at the start of their senior year. Her uncle had tolerated her relationship with Jefferson, whose mother came from old Boston money, but when Uncle Ronan had discovered her pregnancy before she'd been able to escape to college, he had exploded. Since she'd still been a minor, having skipped two grades in elementary school, he could control her movements by simply denying his permission as her legal guardian for her to attend school in person. She had switched to an online university and completed her first year at home, largely confined to her room because of her expanding belly.

She shook her head to clear away the memories and instead pulled open the bottom drawer and lifted folders until she spied the plastic bag with Ethan's bloody sock. She had fished the sock out of her trash from when she treated his puncture wound but hadn't the courage to send it off with her DNA to see if she was his mother. While Ethan's birthdate was a day later from what her uncle had informed her had been her baby's birthday, Ronan might have fudged the date, so using DNA would provide the most definitive answer. Part of her longed to know, but fear at hearing she wasn't made her hesitate.

She let the folders drop over the bag, then shut the drawer. Call Jefferson, then go home to Willoughby and reheated leftovers. Without giving herself a chance to chicken out again, she dialed his number on the office phone. It rang once, twice, three times, then Jefferson's voice filled her ear.

"Hello?"

"Jefferson," she stumbled over his first name, then added quickly, "Mr. Smith, it's Dr. Davenport."

"What can I do for you?"

The cool greeting sent her emotions into a tailspin, but she straightened her shoulders. This wasn't a social call, this was business. "My office manager, Lily Turnbolt, has been trying to reach you about Ethan's insurance."

"Oh, right. Sorry. I had a big order to finish and figured I could return her call next week."

"Usually that would be fine," Eve concurred, "but we have an audit coming up, and we need to make sure our books are in order without any outstanding balances or claims."

"Understood."

Eve waited, but Jefferson didn't add anything else. "Ms. Turnbolt told me she called the insurance company today and was told Ethan's insurance had lapsed."

"I think I must have kept the old card. I'll call first thing Monday with the new insurance info."

"You can give it to me now if that's easier." The words popped out before Eve had time to consider.

"I suppose that will work." His tone said he wasn't happy about being on the phone longer, but Eve couldn't retract her offer now. Lily would appreciate not having to wait for Jefferson to call in with the new insurance info. "Give me a second to get my wallet. I'm in my workshop."

"Sure, I have to get the form from the front desk anyway." She should have thought about that before she called him. "I'll put you on a brief hold."

She did so without waiting for his confirmation, then darted out of her office to the reception area. She found the patient intake form, jotted down Ethan's name at the top, then punched in the button to release the hold on the front desk phone. "I'm back."

"I've got the right insurance card. Ready?"

For the next few minutes, she filled in the requisite insurance data, then verified the info with Jefferson. "Thank you for taking care of this now."

"You're welcome." His voice sounded a bit less frosty, so she chanced a more personal question.

"How's Ethan doing?"

"Oh, he's been fine."

"No lingering effects from the kidnapping attempt?"

"None that I can tell. He loves telling how he escaped."

"It is rather dramatic," Eve agreed, "but I'm glad he's okay. Any news?"

"The police haven't said if there is. Do you have every-thing you need?"

The question caught her off guard, then she remembered he was referring to the health insurance and the reason for her call. "Yes."

"I have to deliver this table and chairs, then pick up Ethan from a friend's."

"Of course." Eve swallowed her hurt at the clipped words. He hadn't contacted her since Ethan's aborted kidnapping, so why would she think he'd want to prolong their talk?

Something ruffled the hairs on the back of her neck, diverting her attention from the conversation with Jefferson. She half-turned as the presence of someone behind her registered.

But it wasn't Lily or another staff member standing there. Instead, she stared into dark, glittering eyes as an intruder, the rest of his face hidden behind a black ski mask, fastened his hands around her neck and squeezed.

CHAPTER

SIX

Jefferson had been about to hang up, miffed that Eve hadn't responded to his farewell when she gasped, then a loud clatter had him pulling his phone away from his ear. He quickly replaced it, his heart revving. "Eve?"

No answer, but more scuffling sounds had him racing out of the detached garage he used as a workshop and into his house for the landline phone he had installed on the advice of the real estate agent who had sold him the home. "There are these weird little pockets of dead cell service around your home, so I recommend you have a landline phone as a back-up," she'd told him. Jefferson had almost ignored her recommendation, but now he was glad he hadn't because it allowed him to call 911 while keeping the cell line open between him and Eve.

While he waited for a dispatcher to pick up, he once again said Eve's name. The only response was a louder crash, then an indistinct voice shouted something in another language, Spanish maybe.

"911, where's your emergency?"

"Twin Oaks Pediatrics. Someone's attacking Dr. Eve Davenport in reception." He kept his cell glued to his right ear while relaying the pertinent info to the dispatcher. After making sure law enforcement and an ambulance were on the way, he disconnected from the landline and jumped into his SUV to head to the clinic. He connected his phone to the vehicle's Bluetooth and gunned the engine. *Please God, let Eve be okay.*

He alternated between praying for Eve's safety and berating his reaction to distance himself after Ethan's kidnapping at the nature center. Her insistence Donahue had something to do with the incidents brought up the past and all his insecurities and hurt about Eve's actions with his brother at prom and with giving away Ethan. Instead of using the kidnapping opportunity to tell her about George's request, he'd avoided her rather than chance her rejection of Ethan again. While Ethan wasn't his son, he loved the boy as his own. He might tell himself it was because Ethan was his twin's son, but his heart whispered it was because Ethan was also Eve's son, the girl he couldn't forget.

"Someone there?"

The woman's accented English accelerated his heartrate even more as he gunned the engine through a yellow light. "Where's Dr. Davenport?"

"She's here and okay. The man, he is gone."

Relief coursed through him, but he wanted—no needed—to hear her voice before he would believe it. "Can you put her on the phone?"

"Yes, here she is."

The brief sound of the phone being transferred, then Eve said, "Jefferson?"

Her husky tone drove his concern even higher. What had happened? He voiced that very question as he stopped for a red light three blocks from the clinic.

"A man." She coughed, then tried again in a whisper. "He tried to strangle me."

"What?" He whipped the vehicle right, needing to be

moving toward Eve and not sitting at a traffic light. He braked briefly at an all-way stop, then swung left on a side street.

"He..." Eve had another coughing fit, this one lasting longer.

The other woman murmured something Jefferson couldn't hear, then she came on the line. "Dr. Eve can't talk right now."

"Tell her I'm a block away." Sirens punctuated the early evening air as Jefferson made the final turn into the parking lot of the small practice. He grabbed his phone and raced for the front door as a police cruiser roared into the lot.

A woman wearing a Clean 4 U yellow vest yanked open the door. "Mr. Smith? Dr. Eve's in here."

Jefferson slipped past her as she presumably waited for the officer to approach, glad Eve had told the woman to allow him entrance. In one of the waiting room chairs, Eve sat with her head bowed over a bottle of water. "Eve!"

She lifted her head. Her pale face and the red marks around her neck fanned his fear for her—and ignited his anger that someone would try to snuff out her life. A tear streaked down her cheek, and he tamped down his ire and rushed to her side.

"Are you okay?" A silly question, given the circumstances, but he had to say something, or other words might pop out, words his heart urged him to say but his head shouted caution. Seeing Eve so vulnerable brought to the forefront his protective nature and his adolescent feelings for the girl who had stolen his heart. In this moment, the truth he'd never stopped loving Eve hit him squarely in the chest with enough force he would have staggered if he hadn't been seated beside her.

She shivered and swayed toward him. He slipped an arm around her shoulder, and she collapsed into his embrace. Holding her close, he was transported back to the numerous times she'd needed comfort during their senior year. He suddenly realized with the clarity of an adult his assumption had been her concerns centered around school, but she'd never actually told him so. What if she had been dealing with something that had happened at home and he'd been oblivious? Eve had rarely talked about her aunt and uncle, hardly ever invited Jefferson to her house. She'd much preferred hanging out at his with George and his parents. Now as he viewed those interactions through the lens of her words about Donahue's potential involvement in the Irish mob, Jefferson wondered what he had missed. He berated himself for not pressing her back then to tell him why she needed comfort. Sure, he'd been a high school senior with his eyes on life after graduation, but still, he could have tried harder. Maybe if he had, things would have turned out differently.

A man dressed in a dark suit approached. "Dr. Davenport?"

Eve lifted her head off his shoulder, dislodging his grip. His arms felt empty without her in them, and he crossed them to avoid reaching for her again.

After introducing himself as Detective Feingold, he said, "Would you tell me what happened?"

Eve sipped from the water bottle. "I was talking on the desk phone to Jefferson, Mr. Smith, about his son's health insurance when a man wearing a black ski mask came up behind me and tried to strangle me."

Her hoarse voice gave credence to her tale, as she spoke of struggling to fend off her attacker as he squeezed his hands around her throat. Only the appearance of Maria Velasquez, the overnight cleaner, saved her life. Maria hit the man with a broom, which caused him to break his hold on Eve. The attacker shoved Maria into her cart, then ran for the back door and disappeared into the night.

Across the room, another officer spoke with Maria, who gesticulated with her hands as she talked. Jefferson shuddered as the realization of how close Eve came to losing her life hit him afresh. He'd dismissed Eve's suggestion her uncle was behind the attacks, but now that she had been assaulted, it was something Jefferson could no longer discount.

"Do you have any idea why someone would want to hurt you?" Feingold asked.

Eve shook her head as a pair of EMTs entered the office. One headed toward Maria and the other to Eve. Feingold closed her notebook as the EMT set down her bag on the floor in front of Eve. "I'll get out of their way."

Jefferson followed the detective, needing to tell him about the kidnapping attempts of his son. "Detective Feingold? There's something you should know."

"What's that?" He paused a short distance from Eve, who had tilted her head back to allow a female EMT to examine her throat. The vivid red marks, some already darkening, sickened him.

Quickly, he told the detective about the two separate kidnapping attempts and the brick through Eve's window.

"You think those are related to tonight's assault on Dr. Davenport?"

Jefferson glanced over his shoulder at Eve, who held an ice pack to her injured throat. When it had only been his son in physical danger, the decision to keep Ethan's parentage a secret had seemed a no brainer, but in light of Eve's assault, the stakes had changed. Someone could be trying to get to Ethan through his mother, who was listed on his birth certificate as Eve Donahue. But he also didn't want to reveal the information since Eve had chosen to keep her motherhood hidden. Everywhere he'd gone, people had sung the praises of Dr. Eve Davenport. Hearing she'd given up her baby at birth might damage her reputation and her medical practice.

"Mr. Smith?"

Feingold's prompt pushed him to reveal at least part of

the secret. "I, well, you see, Ethan is really my nephew, the son of my brother, George."

The detective frowned. "You think your brother might be behind the attempts to get Ethan back?"

"My twin brother, but no, George couldn't." Jefferson swallowed the lump that clogged his throat whenever he thought about his sibling. "Because George died last year in a car accident."

"What about the child's mother?"

He summoned his courage, knowing he was about to rip the bandage off Eve's secret, but he could no longer justify keeping the identity under wraps, given the escalation of the attacks. "It's Dr. Davenport."

Feingold tilted his head as if not sure he'd heard Jefferson correctly. "Dr. Davenport is Ethan's mother?"

"Yes."

A loud gasp had him whirling around in time to see Eve collapse into a heap on the floor, her white face in stark contrast to the red streaks on her neck.

EVE MOANED, THEN WISHED SHE HADN'T AS PAIN SEARED HER throat. Memories of the assault surfaced in her scrambled brain. The sensation of lying on the floor, a light blanket over her, puzzled her until the recollection of Jefferson's stark words had her mind whirring. Ethan was her son.

Her son.

The baby she'd thought was dead was alive.

Tears leaked out of her eyes, trailing down her cheeks. Tears of joy and sorrow. Joy because the child she thought she would never hold in her arms was living. Sorrow for missing out on Ethan's first eight years of life. She breathed a prayer of thanksgiving to God for this miracle of restoration, battling back the questions of why and how that tried to crowd in. For a few minutes, she wanted to focus on how grateful she was to have the chance to know her son—her little boy—after living with regret and guilt for years.

"Dr. Davenport?"

She pried her eyes open to meet the concerned gaze of Tamisan, the EMT who had treated her injury only a few minutes earlier. At least, Eve hoped she had only been unconscious for a little while.

"Nice to have you back among the living." Tamisan patted Eve's shoulder. "Just rest here for a minute."

"Is Jefferson—Mr. Smith—still here?" Eve winced as talking exacerbated her sore throat.

"If you mean the handsome man with the beard, then I'm not sure." Tamisan craned her neck. "I don't see him in the waiting area."

More tears streamed down Eve's cheeks. "I don't know why I'm turning on the waterworks."

"You've had a big shock." Tamisan considered her, then added, "Two big shocks, if I'm not mistaken."

Eve didn't know how to respond, not when she had a million questions only Jefferson could answer, starting with why had he and George kept Ethan from her all these years. She hadn't changed her name until medical school six years ago. Tamisan helped Eve into a purple plastic chair, draping the emergency blanket around her shoulders. The EMT recommended Eve follow up with her primary care physician in the morning, then left.

Detective Feingold returned her side. "You okay, Dr. Davenport?"

"I've been better," Eve croaked. "In shock, mostly."

"Because of the attack?" The detective assessed her, his gaze not giving away what he thought about the town's leading pediatrician leaving her child to be raised by his father. Because that's exactly what it looked like to an outsider—Eve had abandoned her baby in pursuit of her own career.

But Eve hadn't survived living under her uncle's roof without developing a backbone of steel, able to withstand fierce storms, so she squared her shoulders. "That contributed to it, but it's mostly finding out the baby I thought had died was alive. Is, in fact, Ethan Smith."

"You didn't know Ethan was your son?"

"No." Eve bit her lip. "I did wonder when Ethan let slip about George, Jefferson's twin brother, was his first dad, but I hadn't asked Jefferson directly about it."

Feingold consulted his notebook. "Mr. Smith said something about a shamrock and your uncle being in the Irish mob?"

Eve darted a glance around the room, but again couldn't spot Jefferson. "Where is Mr. Smith?"

"He and an officer went to pick up Ethan from a classmate's home."

Made sense Jefferson would want to ensure Ethan was safe. Between sips of water from a bottle the officer handed her, Eve related what little she suspected about her uncle's involvement in the Irish mob, then told about shamrock sightings on the wannabe kidnappers and the brick.

Feingold listened attentively, jotting things down in his notebook. "Why would your uncle want to harm you or the boy?"

"I don't know." Eve furrowed her brow as a memory of her attacker surfaced. "Wait, I remembered something." She closed her eyes to bring the moment into clarity. "The man who tried to strangle me said something about how the brat would be taken care of too."

Eve sucked in a deep breathe despite the pain in her throat, glad to be able to breath easily without the man's hands around her neck. Since childhood, she had always had a deep-seated fear of not being able to breath, and now she strained to not let that fear overcome her.

"By *the brat*, you think he meant Ethan?"

"Who else? While I know a lot of the town's children because of my job, there's no one I'm close to. With Ethan being my son," Eve couldn't suppress the thrill of those words, "it's logical to assume my assailant meant Ethan."

"We'll keep that in mind." The detective stood. "I will be in touch with the Boston PD to see what they can tell me about Ronan Donahue. In the meantime, we will step up patrols by the clinic and yours and Mr. Smith's homes."

Eve knew the small police force hadn't the manpower to assign a full-time bodyguard, so she thanked the detective and went to her office to gather her things. The police sent Maria home to allow forensics to complete their work. Eve nodded to the officer, who headed to his patrol car when she went to hers. She had to see Ethan before she went to her house despite her body sagging with tiredness.

Once at Jefferson's home, she parked behind another patrol car and hustled up the walk before she could talk herself out of the visit. She rang the doorbell and waited, second guessing her decision with each second that passed. She had turned to go, convinced Jefferson wouldn't answer the door, when he opened it.

"Eve, what are you doing here?" Jefferson dried his hands on a dishtowel.

"I shouldn't have dropped by without calling first, but I had to see Ethan after..." Tears once more spilled down her cheeks. She pitched her voice lower. "He's my son? Truly?"

A frown pulled the corners of Jefferson's mouth down. "I don't have time to play games with you."

The anger behind his words slapped her in the face. "Games? I'm not playing games. I didn't know, Uncle Ronan told me, I mean, I thought..." She put a hand over her mouth as Ethan skidded into view.

"Dr. Davenport!" He squeezed under his father's arm to stand in front of her.

Eve drank in his appearance, his blue eyes the same shade as her mother's in the few photos she had of her parents. His tousled hair the same texture and shade of her own locks.

"Hey, why's your neck all red?"

She yanked her attention back to the child. "I tied my scarf too tight and look what happened."

"Weird." He leaned around her and pointed toward the curb. "Why is there a police car, no, two police cars, in front of our house?"

"Enough questions. They're probably wondering why you're not in bed," Jefferson said. "Let's go."

"Aw, Dad. Do I hafta?"

"Yes, now, young man. Go brush your teeth and get into your pj's. I'll be up in five minutes to tuck you in."

Ethan huffed but trudged off. Before Jefferson could shut the door in her face, Eve gave into temptation. "Can I tuck him in tonight?" She longed to participate in the rituals of parenthood, to start to make up for all the nights she hadn't been there to say goodnight to her son.

"No."

Jefferson's short reply doused the hope that had sprouted in her heart, but she wasn't going to give up her dream so easily. "Why not?"

"You've been through a lot tonight. I think it's best that you go home and rest, and we'll talk about this later." He crossed his arms, signaling he wasn't going to budge.

Eve wasn't either. Every fiber of her being wanted to be near Ethan. "But he's my son, and I want to be part of his life."

Jefferson stepped closer, the ire in his eyes flashing red hot. "You can't pick and choose when you want to be a mother—it's a lifelong commitment."

"I know that." She swiped at the moisture on her cheeks

with the back of her hand. "I wouldn't say anything about who I am. It's obvious he doesn't know I'm his mother."

"He doesn't, and I see no need to change that now."

The implacable set of his jaw made her swallow her other arguments. She would retreat for now, but if Jefferson thought he had won the battle, he was sorely mistaken.

"Dr. Davenport!"

Eve turned as one of the patrol officers ran up from his patrol vehicle, his radio squawking.

"Your cabin's on fire!"

SEVEN

"No!" Eve hadn't meant to shout, but the news shook her. "Willoughby's inside!"

"There's someone in your house?" The officer, whose name she'd forgotten, spoke in code into his shoulder mic. "Where is the person?"

"Not a person. My cat." She sucked in a breath but couldn't calm her shudders.

The patrolman relayed the info, then gestured toward his vehicle. "I'll drive you to the house."

"Thanks." Once in the front seat of the cruiser, Eve glanced back at Jefferson's house. He stood silhouetted in the doorway, his face in shadow. Probably glad she was leaving. She scrubbed her hands over her face to brush away yet more tears. She hadn't cried this much since she'd been expecting Ethan, but then again, she hadn't experienced this much stress since that time either. She'd always been a crier, which her uncle had hated. Eve had learned fast how to hide her tears from her aunt and uncle, who equated sniffling with weakness.

Soon the cruiser pulled over to the side of the short road

leading to her cabin, unable to go further because of the emergency vehicles clogging the lane. Smoke billowed toward the first stars twinkling in the heavens. Usually, gazing through her telescope to find constellations soothed her after a long day at the office, but likely the hungry flames had gobbled up her telescope along with the rest of her possessions. She exited the vehicle and jogged through the emergency personnel roaming about in what appeared to be organized chaos but in reality what was synchronized movements with the aim of putting out the fire.

As she rounded the bend, another cry of despair escaped her at the greedy flames licking the wooden frame of her snug abode. Firefighters aimed streams of water at the house, while another group doused the nearby trees and vegetation to prevent a wildfire from igniting.

"Ma'am, you can't be here." A firefighter, his face blackened with soot, blocked her path.

"I'm the homeowner." She choked as a breeze carried smoke into her space, but she wasn't leaving until she knew the fate of Willoughby. "My cat?"

The man's stance relaxed a fraction. "Over there," he pointed toward an ambulance where a firefighter in full gear stood talking to someone in the open back bay.

"Thanks." Eve hustled over. "Excuse me? I'm looking for my cat."

The firefighter stepped back, allowing Eve to see an EMT holding Willoughby wrapped in a towel like a burrito with only his head peeking out. He meowed as if sensing Eve was near.

"Willoughby!" She rushed to her furry companion, thankful the fire hadn't consumed him like it was eating her home. "Is he okay?"

The EMT transferred the cat to Eve's arms. "I think so. He's a bit singed but hasn't been coughing too much. He'll need lots of water, and, if you could manage to give him a bath, that would help remove the soot still on his fur."

She hugged the feline to her chest. "I have no idea whether he'll tolerate a bath or not. Thank you for rescuing him."

The firefighter grinned. "We always like a happy ending, at least for our furry friend here. Our truck arrived first, and we saw your cat sticker on the front door alerting us about the pet. Luckily, the fire hadn't spread too badly to the front, so we were able to get the door open. This guy shot out like a cannon, and Allie here managed to coax him out of the woods a little while ago."

"Thank you," Eve told the EMT as the firefighter returned to his crew.

"Dr. Davenport?"

Clutching Willoughby, Eve pivoted to meet the fire chief, Susan Blathers, whose twin boys were her patients.

"Good news is that the fire is nearly out and we were able to stop it from spreading to the woods." Exhaustion mixed with soot on the older woman's face. "I'm glad we were able get your cat out safely."

"Me too." Eve hugged the cat, eliciting a meow from Willoughby. "Any idea how it started?"

"From what my firefighters are reporting, the fire spread fast, which usually means an accelerant."

The words should have made sense, but Eve couldn't put them in context. An accelerant meant... "You think someone deliberately set my house on fire?"

Susan nodded. "I do, but until the arson investigator comes in the morning to take a closer look, it's pure speculation on my part."

Eve stared at her smoldering home, which had been her safe haven for three years. She stroked Willoughby's head, the fur not as silky as usual given the soot clinging to the hair.

"I heard about the assault earlier tonight." Susan laid a hand on her arm. "I'm so sorry you have the fire to contend with on top of everything else."

Eve wasn't surprised Susan had been informed about the assault. Her throat ached despite the over-the-counter pain medication she'd taken before heading to Jefferson's house. She'd been looking forward to crashing in her own bed, but now she would need to find a place for her and Willoughby to stay.

As if reading her thoughts, Susan added, "I'd invite you to stay with us, but Chet's allergic to cats, and I know you don't want to be separated from your friend."

"Thanks, but I can ask Isabelle if she has any room at the B&B." Her friend wouldn't mind Willoughby's presence either.

"Oh, didn't you hear? The Twin Oaks B&B has been completely taken over by the Harrisons and their family reunion—Alec and Isabelle even gave up their apartment for the group. They went to stay with her parents and are only coming back in the mornings to fix breakfast and check the rooms."

While glad their business had such a lucrative booking, it meant she was back to square one in finding a place to stay.

"She can stay with me."

Eve whirled around at the sound of Jefferson's voice. Willoughby squawked at her tight grip, and she loosened her hold a fraction. She didn't see Ethan, and her heart pounded with fear that Jefferson had left him alone—an irrational thought, given how protective of the child Jefferson had been.

"Ethan's in bed, and I called to see if the officer outside our house could sit inside so I could check on you."

Her shoulders relaxed at the news a police officer was guarding Ethan, but it still didn't relay why he'd come to see her house burn. Even more puzzling was his offer of a place to stay, especially after he'd made it clear she wasn't welcome a little while ago.

"I'm Jefferson Smith, Ethan's father." Jefferson thrust his hand toward Susan, who introduced herself after throwing Eve a we'll-talk-later look.

"Sounds like you've got someplace to go with your cat," Susan said. "I'm going to check on the status."

The fire chief strode away before Eve could think of a reason to keep her around. Alone with Jefferson, he reiterated his offer. "You can stay in the spare room. Ethan will be thrilled to have Willoughby to play with too."

"Are you sure that's okay? I might have a conversation or two with Ethan when you're not around."

The tips of Jefferson's ears reddened, a sign her snark had hit its intended mark. But she refused to feel bad about the remark, given his treatment of her earlier—and his keeping Ethan's parentage a secret from her. "Yes. Is there a place to get some cat supplies?"

She'd forgotten all she had was the cat wrapped in a towel and nothing else. "What time is it?"

"Nine."

"The only place open is the Walmart over in Staunton, and that's forty minutes away." Weariness swept over her, and her knees wobbled. Jefferson encircled her from behind with his arms, keeping her and Willoughby upright. "Hey, it's okay. You've had quite the night."

The tears she had been fighting to keep at bay since arriving to see her house aflame broke through her defenses and streamed down her cheeks. "Who is doing this to me, to Ethan? And why? I don't understand any of it. I thought moving away from Boston and changing my name would mean my uncle would leave me alone. He has, but this feels personal. It's not random. Now that I know Ethan is my son, then it must be my uncle who's behind it. Because who else would target both me and Ethan?"

Jefferson handed Eve a mug of hot chocolate. One of the police officers had called the local animal shelter owner and managed to get some emergency supplies of cat litter and box, plus some food, so they didn't have to make the long trek to Walmart right away. Willoughby was locked in the guest room with an attached bathroom off the living room. He hadn't furnished it yet, but did have a twin-size air mattress and extra linens, which Eve proclaimed good enough for a couple of nights.

"Thank you for putting us up. It will only be a for a few days." Eve sipped her cocoa as she sank deeper into the couch in front of the fire. Seeing her shivering after settling her cat had him building the fire and making the hot beverage for her.

The low light from the contained flames and a single lamp burning on the end table cast her face in shadows, softening the marks from the assault. He peeked outside to check that the patrol car was still stationed there before taking a seat on the other end of the sofa.

"Why didn't you tell me Ethan was my son?"

He'd been expecting questions, since he'd fobbed her off earlier, but this one reignited his frustration. "Why are you pretending you didn't know he was?"

"What are you talking about?"

The bewilderment in her question should have made him pause, but years of anger at her heartless actions spilled over. "You sent your uncle to dump the baby off at our house with instructions never to bother you again about his upbringing."

Eve's hand jerked, jostling cocoa out of the mug. She set it down on the coffee table, wiping her hand down the side of her jeans, then turned to face him to repeat her earlier question. "What are you talking about?"

"Stop it, Eve." He stood to pace in front of the fireplace.

"Stop pretending you have no idea when it was all your idea to send the baby to us so you could pursue your medical career. How ironic you specialized in pediatrics when you didn't even want your own kid."

She bowed her head, but he wasn't going to let her come up with a plausible story like she'd done as a teenager, making his family feel sorry for her and the way Donahue kept such close tabs on her.

"Donahue told us all about how you lied about everything. The way you would tell people how terrible he treated you when all he did was bring you to live with him and his wife after your parents were killed in a car accident and left you with nothing. He sat there in my parents' living room, tears in his eyes, as he relayed how you'd said you wanted nothing to do with Ethan and to never contact you again."

When she stayed silent, he lashed out. "George isn't here to get the answers he wanted, that we all wanted, but I think you owe me the truth."

She leapt to her feet, her entire body shaking. "The truth? You wouldn't believe me if I told you."

"Try me."

For a moment, they locked gazes, the heat of their combined anger warming the space between them. Then she closed her eyes and drew in a deep breath, letting it out slowly and diffusing some of the tension simmering in the room. She hugged her arms around her waist, turning her face toward the fire crackling in the hearth. "The truth is, my uncle is the liar, spinning stories to cover his actions."

Her voice dropped to a near whisper but in the stillness of the night, Jefferson easily heard her.

"He didn't take me in by the kindness of his heart—he did it for the insurance money from my parents' estate. When I was applying to medical school, I found out he had been appointed my guardian and thus had control over the money since I was a minor. I never saw a penny of the nearly $5 million their combined life insurance policies paid. He and my aunt Lorraine never wanted kids, which they made no secret about. I always felt like I was in the way. I could give you example upon example of how terrible they treated me, but here's one. You know how I always helped clear trays for everyone in the lunchroom?"

Jefferson nodded, an image of the young Eve juggling several plastic trays filled with uneaten food filling his mind.

"I did it because my uncle refused to give me lunch money or let me pack a lunch."

He frowned. "Why would he do that?"

She shrugged. "I couldn't tell you, but I suspect it was to show me who was in control—and it wasn't me."

He couldn't square that with the man who so generously gave to charities, including the area food bank.

As if sensing his disbelief, Eve added, "You and George and the others used to tease me that I wasn't eating lunch because I wanted to stay thin, but the reality was I wasn't eating lunch because I had no lunch to eat. The only way I could find something to eat was if I grabbed some of the uneaten food off trays, and the only way to do that was by clearing them myself."

"But you could have told someone, and they would have given you cereal to eat. They don't let kids go hungry." He recalled that much, having forgotten his own lunch or money a time or two.

"I tried that in elementary school. When my uncle found out, he withheld breakfast and only gave me one slice of bread and water for dinner for a week. So I switched to saying I wasn't hungry." She shrugged. "Not many people noticed I never ate, and those that did assumed it was a choice."

Jefferson opened his mouth to lambast her version of events, still not convinced Donahue could have treated his own niece with such cold-heartedness, but she held up her hand as if to stem his words.

"Please don't defend him. You only saw what he wanted you to see, the perfect public face he showed the world. You can believe me or not. As for Ethan." Her voice trembled and she cleared her throat.

Then the lights went out.

EIGHT

J efferson raced for the stairs, his only thought Ethan's safety and how his son hated to be in the dark. He slept with two nightlights plugged into separate wall outlets to illuminate more of his room. At Ethan's door, he paused, not wanting to scare his son if Ethan hadn't awoken.

"Do you lose power regularly?" Eve's soft question startled him, as he hadn't realized she'd followed him up the stairs.

"Not recently, as I thought I had fixed the problem with the wiring." The 125-year-old house had been owned for the past fifty years by an old bachelor who had fancied himself a DIYer. Jefferson had gotten the property, which included a large, heated barn, for a song but had spent a pretty penny addressing all the "fixes" the previous owner had done. After blowing fuses anytime more than one thing had been plugged in at a time, he'd had an electrician out to untangle the wiring situation, but perhaps something had been overlooked.

He pressed his ear closer to Ethan's door. Silence. Still, he wouldn't be satisfied unless he saw his son sleeping peacefully. Easing open the door, he breathed a sigh of relief as

Ethan stirred but didn't awaken. He should check on the fuse box in the basement, but he was reluctant to leave Ethan alone.

Stepping back into the hallway, he pulled the door nearly closed. "Would you wait here while I check on why the power went out?"

"Of course." She patted her back pocket. "Got my phone with me. I'll wait right here until you come back."

"Thank you. I'll text the officer outside what's going on before I head down to the basement to look at the fuse box."

"Good plan."

Her approval pleased him more than it should have, but he hadn't time to delve into his jumbled feelings for Dr. Eve Davenport, not when danger stalked her and Ethan like a lion after its dinner. He hustled down the stairs and grabbed his phone off the end table where he'd forgotten it in his haste to check on his son. He texted the officer outside, then decided to wait for his reply before checking the fuse box. Nothing. Jefferson moved to the living room's big bay window, positioning himself along the wall to peer out through the open wooden slats.

No patrol car was parked along the curb. Unease prickled the back of his neck. He brought up Detective Feingold's number and hit call. It rang several times before the man answered by barking out his rank and last name.

"Jefferson Smith here. I'm sorry to bother you so late, but Dr. Davenport and her cat are staying with me since the house fire." Jefferson assumed the detective would have heard about the fire and plowed on. "But the lights went out, and the officer who had been sitting outside my house is no longer there."

"Are the windows and doors locked?"

"Yes, the officer checked the house before he returned to his car a few hours ago." Jefferson paced back to the bottom of the stairs, but no one stirred.

"Anyone else on your block lose electricity?"

Jefferson returned to the front window and spied lights on across the street. "The house across from us has lights." He craned his neck and glimpsed lights burning in the upstairs windows of the house to his right and informed the detective.

"I don't like this, given the earlier attacks and the fire at Dr. Davenport's home. Have you checked your fuse box?"

"I haven't because it's in the basement and I wanted to let the officer outside know what was happening first."

"Can you block access to the basement?"

Jefferson moved toward the kitchen. "I can lock the door."

"Do it. I'm sending the closest patrol car there now—should arrive in five minutes. I'll be there in ten."

Jefferson thanked him, then bolted the basement door. He double-checked the back door with its dead bolt and all the downstairs windows, plus the front door before going back upstairs. Eve sat with her back against the wall to the right of Ethan's door. He quietly filled her in on what the detective said, then returned to wait at the bottom of the stairs for the police to arrive.

Soon his phone buzzed with the news from the detective that two patrol cars had arrived and the officers would check the outside of the house first. Less than five minutes later, Detective Feingold texted to say he was at the front door with the officers.

Jefferson let them inside, then retreated upstairs to wait with Eve. He wasn't willing to leave Ethan's side, not until they knew what had happened to the power. Then brightness filled the house as the lights came back on. He must have flipped the wall switch automatically when racing to check on Ethan.

Beside him, Eve pressed her fingers into her temples. "At least the lights are back on."

"Yeah." He rose and offered her his hand.

She hesitated, then placed her hand in his. The softness of

her skin contrasted with the callouses on his finger pads and palms from his woodworking tools. With a tug, he pulled her to her feet, but he must have put more effort into it than he'd intended because she stumbled into his chest.

His arms went around her, cradling her against him. "Easy there."

Eve shuddered in his embrace, a quiet sniffle sending his senses into overdrive. The Eve he remembered rarely showed any emotion, and he'd only seen her cry once, the morning he'd broken up with her. She couldn't seem to catch her breath, or perhaps she was trying to stem tears. "It's okay."

"But," she hiccuped, "it's not. Someone's trying to hurt me and Ethan, and my house is toast, and…"

"Shhh." He gently pressed her head toward his shoulder, his fingers tangling with her hair while he rubbed her back. "I've got you."

Eve's arms came around his waist, her sobs muffled by his chest. For a few minutes, they stood in the hallway while she cried.

Detective Feingold appeared at the foot of the stairs. To his credit, he didn't comment on Jefferson holding Eve so close. "I'll wait in the kitchen."

Jefferson nodded to let the detective know he'd heard him.

Eve pushed back from his chest, breaking his hold. "I'm sorry."

"No need. It's been quite the day."

"Was that the detective?"

"He's waiting for us in the kitchen."

She shoved a hand through her hair, sending the strands every which way. Jefferson stopped himself from reaching out to smooth it back down. He might have offered her comfort, but she still hadn't adequately explained why she'd abandoned her baby.

"I'll meet you there after I splash some water on my face." She disappeared downstairs.

Jefferson checked on Ethan once more, his son's face now bathed in the glow from the two nightlights. He took a moment to pray for Ethan's protection—and for his own heart to withstand the temptation to fall in love with Eve Davenport again.

Eve flipped to her back, dislodging Willoughby from his place snug against her side. The cat meowed and stalked off the mattress, finally having enough of her restless sleeping. Or not sleeping. Detective Feingold had reported the officers had discovered several blown fuses. A call to the electrician who had completed the work last week had ferreted out the problem—he'd not replaced the old fuses with new ones, having used the old ones as placeholders when doing the work. He promised to come out first thing in the morning to take care of it.

Meanwhile, the officer who had been outside their house had responded to a convenience store robbery a few blocks away and had been reprimanded for leaving his post without alerting Jefferson or his supervisor at the station. Eve had been reassured that the electricity outage had been a coincidence, and no one appeared to have blamed Jefferson for being overly cautious in bringing in the cops. She hadn't been pleased to learn the fire marshal was treating the fire at her home as suspected arson, with an investigator coming out soon to start sifting through the damage to pinpoint the source. Her mind kept circling back to her uncle as being behind the attacks, but she couldn't figure out why he would do so.

Her brain refused to turn off as more questions crowded in from all angles, the utmost ones centering around how Jefferson would react when she told him her version of what had happened when Ethan was born. Would he continue to be skeptical, or would he see the truth in her words? His tenderness in comforting her when she broke down and cried gave her a sliver of hope he wouldn't dismiss her tale as outright fiction, but even if he believed her, he might not agree to let her be part of Ethan's life.

While she longed to be more than the child's doctor and occasional visitor, she wasn't sure she deserved to be his mother. After all, she should have fought harder to discover what happened to him, to ask more questions rather than accept her aunt and uncle's version of events. There was only so much blame she could avoid by her status as a sheltered sixteen-year-old—there came a time when she should have verified what they said happened had occurred. She who knew how they lied had never questioned their story about Ethan's birth.

Sleep continued to elude her, and after another hour of tossing and turning, she decided she might as well get up. Four-thirty wasn't too early. During her residency, she often worked for twenty-four hours straight. Some good, strong coffee might kickstart her brain into something more productive than endless questions.

She slipped back into her jeans, having taken them off to sleep. Later this morning, she would grab some fresh clothes from the stash she kept at the office and in the trunk of her car, a habit she'd gotten into during medical school and one she was glad she hadn't discontinued. For now, yesterday's clothes would have to do.

In the kitchen, she found ground coffee and Jefferson's French press. Soon the scent of coffee filled the kitchen. She poured the first cup black and sat down at the kitchen table, glad she'd had her laptop in her car and not at her house, where she usually left it. Powering it up, she decided to see what she could find out about her parents, Maeve and Nigel Brandt. Her name had been chosen because it was part of her mother's first name. Maeve had been Ronan Donahue's younger sister, the only children of Kagen and Edana Donahue, whom Eve had never met. She started by Googling "Kagen and Edana Donahue and Boston," since her uncle had said he'd grown up in the city.

To her surprise, the first articles that popped up were about a horrendous house fire that killed Kagen and Edana, leaving Ronan and Maeve orphans. Eve vaguely recalled asking her uncle about some scarring on his left arm and being told he'd gotten burned as a teenager. Maybe that had happened in the same fire that killed his parents. She clicked on one of the articles, which speculated on the cause of the fire. Only the parents had been home at the time, as the two teenagers had been staying over at a friends' home. A short article written a few weeks later indicated the cause of the fire couldn't be definitely determined, with a quote from the fire investigator saying he wasn't ruling out arson. She couldn't find any other articles and decided it probably didn't matter.

Next, she Googled her parents' names but found too many returns to sort through. She tried "Maeve and Nigel Brandt and Carmel, Indiana," where she'd been born, and found a link to the vehicle accident that killed them. The top one relayed what Ronan had told her—she had been strapped into her car seat in the back while her father drove and her mother rode shotgun. An intoxicated driver had smashed into their vehicle head-on at a high speed, killing all three adults. She alone had survived, but because the accident occurred on a country road, no one discovered what had happened until the morning. Being only fifteen months old at the time, she had no memory of the events.

"You're up early." Jefferson's sleepy voice from behind her made her jump.

She turned, her hand on her heart. "You startled me."

He smothered a yawn behind his hand. "Sorry, not used to having another adult in the house. Since I'm always trying to get Ethan to sleep later, I tend to tiptoe in the mornings."

The reminder that she'd see her son when he tumbled out of bed brought a smile to her lips. "It's okay. I woke up before five and couldn't get back to sleep."

Jefferson leaned against the counter, having poured himself a cup of coffee from the second carafe she'd made within the last half hour. "You're looking quite chipper for being up for over two hours."

She glanced at the clock. 7:14. "Didn't realize so much time had passed." She lifted her mug. "I've been running on this excellent coffee."

"I get it from a local roaster." Jefferson gestured toward her laptop with his mug. "What has you so engrossed?"

"I couldn't help thinking that since Ethan's my son, the attacks on both of us must be related."

"By your uncle."

She shrugged as if the movement would allow her to ignore his disagreement with her hypothesis. "It's the only thing that makes sense, unless there's something in George's past that would point to these kind of attacks."

He sipped his coffee, his gaze directed toward the worn linoleum floor. She waited, giving the room a closer examination. The kitchen retained a 1970s vibe with its solid wood cabinets and avocado appliances. She'd be surprised if the electric cooktop still worked. The most recent appliance appeared to be the fridge, although its almond color suggested it had been replaced at least three decades ago.

"George had been working on something secretive before his death."

"What was it?" Maybe this had nothing to do with her uncle after all, although from the tension rolling off Jefferson, he wasn't sure about sharing it with her.

"He had already decided not to go to college and applied to the Boston police academy. He'd just been accepted when your uncle showed up with the baby. I was home on spring break from Columbia University."

"Oh, I'm glad you decided to attend." Attending Columbia in New York City had been his dream, and when he'd gotten in, she had been both thrilled and sad, knowing he would not want to continue their relationship long distance, since she had been accepted at Georgetown University in Washington, DC. The baby had derailed her plans, so she was happy to hear he, at least, had been able to fulfill his dream.

"It was only for one year."

Her joy faded at the grim set of his mouth. She forced her lips to form the question to which she feared she knew the answer. "Why?"

"Because of Ethan. Mom and Dad couldn't take care of a baby, not with their full-time jobs, and George couldn't attend the police academy with a baby in tow. To make it work, I agreed to transfer my sophomore year to Boston U and work my class schedule around George's work schedule. In the interim, my mom took a short leave of absence from work because childcare for an infant was too expensive."

She swallowed the bitter taste in her mouth at his words. "I'm so sorry, Jefferson."

"Are you? Because from where I stand, we made all the sacrifices for the baby, and you sailed through college and medical school, finishing everything at the ripe old age of twenty-two. You have a good job in what appears to be a thriving practice, so your pity isn't what I need."

She flinched at the harshness in his tone but refused to absorb his pain. "It must have been hard."

"You bet it was." He stormed out of the kitchen, only to return a short time later. "Ethan's still sleeping. I think it's time you told me exactly why you gave him up."

CHAPTER

NINE

The little color in Eve's cheeks drained away, leaving her skin so pale, he thought he could see the blood vessels. For a few seconds, she didn't speak, then she squared her shoulders as if preparing for battle. The movement touched a long-forgotten memory of how she would do that very action right before she'd walk up the sidewalk to her uncle's house. He'd only been inside the massive house in Southborough twice, despite he and Eve being a couple for most of their senior year, but he recalled how sterile and tomblike the place had struck him. Eve's words last night about the food restrictions Donahue put on her reverberated in his mind, sowing seeds of doubt as to what he thought he knew about Eve. Now, he focused on the story spilling out of her.

"When my uncle discovered I was expecting, he was furious. He tried to get me to agree to an abortion, but I flat out refused. He even made an appointment and took me to a clinic, but when I realized where we were, I said I would scream the house down because I was not killing my baby." Eve kept her head down, her hands cupped around her mug as she sat at the kitchen table. "He believed me because we went home without entering the clinic, then he locked me in my room the entire summer. When he realized I wasn't going to relent, he took me to an OB-GYN for prenatal care, but he made it clear I was not keeping the baby and that he would not support me and an infant in his home."

She paused, as if overcome by the story, which, to Jefferson's mind, still didn't add up to her thrusting the baby upon George and cutting off all contact.

He did have one question that couldn't wait for her narrative to finish. "Why didn't you talk to George about it?" *Or me.*

"He took away my phone, tablet, and computer. The only landline was in his office. He had spies everywhere—the housekeeper, the cook, the grounds men all reported my movements to my uncle. I made it to my neighbor's front door once, hoping Mrs. Crossin would let me use her phone to call you, but my uncle hurried up the walk as she opened the door. He apologized for my disturbing her, and she sympathized with him about 'my condition.'" She barked out a short laugh. "I thought she was referring to my pregnancy, but my uncle informed me later he'd told the neighbors I was suffering from a mental breakdown and not to believe a word I said. Or let me to use a phone."

Jefferson's stomach tightened as she relayed more stories about how Donahue had kept her a virtual prisoner during her pregnancy. Her uncle allowed her to take online classes toward her undergraduate degree, but only if she agreed to use the laptop he provided, which she knew had spyware installed.

"Then the baby came a month early." She shuddered as if remembering the birth. "My uncle and aunt were at some charity function, and I was locked in my room as usual. I pounded on the door, begging for help after my water broke, but the servants had been threatened with their jobs or perhaps even deportation back to their home countries if they disobeyed my uncle's commands."

Horror gripped Jefferson as she told about nearly passing out on the cold tile floor of the adjoining bathroom, then realizing she was bleeding profusely. By the time her uncle and aunt returned, she'd given birth to the baby. "A nurse told me later they thought I wouldn't make it because I'd lost so much blood during the delivery. When I was discharged from the hospital, I couldn't get out of bed for weeks, I was so weak. I had to drop out of school for the semester and retake the classes over the summer."

Jefferson couldn't move as the realization Eve could not have insisted Donahue give the baby to George if she was fighting for her life in the hospital. But later, when she had recovered, why hadn't she come for Ethan? "I'm so sorry. We had no idea Ethan's birth was so traumatic."

"But you're still judging me for not coming for him once I'd recovered, right?" Her tone still held a wealth of pain. "My uncle informed me I would not be leaving the house for my sophomore year of college as I'd thought. Instead, he insisted I continue online schooling, and he kept me locked in my room as before. This time, it was easier to bear because it took months for me to recover from the birth."

She raised her head, the anguish in her eyes so raw, he gasped.

"You see, for many months afterward, I didn't care about school, about leaving the house, about anything because..." Her voice faltered, then she rallied. "Because, you see, once I had returned to the land of the living in the hospital, my uncle informed me the baby had died."

Jefferson stared at her as he processed what she'd said, but even then, he could scarcely believe it. "He said your baby was dead?"

"Yes." Her clipped response made him cringe. "And before you say I should have known or could have somehow found out that wasn't the case, remember he kept me isolated in the hospital and at home. He'd told your family I wanted nothing to do with the baby or them. I already felt so guilty for going into labor four weeks early, then not managing to keep my wits about me while giving birth, so it was easy to believe that the baby hadn't made it. I had no way to know how long I'd passed out on the bathroom floor before help arrived. Maybe I should have questioned his version of events later, but when I had regained some of my strength, he took me to the family cemetery and showed me the baby's grave."

Tears rained down her cheeks as she locked eyes with him. "I was seventeen and all alone. How could I have believed otherwise?"

The truth shining in her eyes slammed him in the gut with the force of a sledgehammer. He, George, and their parents had all believed Donahue's story because Eve wasn't there to contradict him. He recalled how both he and George had tried to call her cell phone only to find out the number had been disconnected. He'd even gone to the house but had been turned away by the housekeeper with the admonishment not to return.

"Eve, I'm so sorry. We had no idea." Jefferson set down his mug. "I—"

A scream split the air, followed by a crash from upstairs. Ethan!

EVE RACED AFTER JEFFERSON AS HE RUSHED FOR THE STAIRS, calling his son's name. Her heart, bruised from retelling the most traumatic event of her life, thudded hard.

At the top of the stairs, Jefferson shouted over his shoulder, "Get the police! Outside!"

Right, the officer in the patrol car in front of the house. She changed directions and flew out of the house and into a light morning drizzle. But at the curb, there was no patrol car. She glanced up and down the street, but no car. Whipping her phone out of her back pocket, she dialed 911 as she headed back inside.

"911, where's your emergency?"

"Jefferson Smith's house on Pine Avenue." She caught a glimpse of the house number beside the front door. "1429."

Yanking open the front door, the sounds of a struggle going on upstairs sent her in that direction. "Hurry, I think there's someone in his son's—our son's—room!" She didn't wait to hear what else the dispatcher said but barreled up the stairs and into Ethan's room.

"You will not take my son!" Jefferson shouted as he hung onto Ethan's legs while a man on a ladder tugged on the boy's torso, which dangled out the window.

She reversed her steps and flew as fast as she could to the kitchen door. She halted before bursting into the backyard, not wanting to startle the man on the ladder trying to kidnap Ethan. Easing open the back door, she moved onto the stoop, then slid down behind the tall evergreen bushes alongside the back of the house. She inched her way closer to the long metal ladder propped against the house, its base leaning against a section of the bushes.

The man at the top of the ladder rained down curses as the precipitation picked up intensity. Another man dressed in dark clothes held the ladder at the base, but his face wasn't completely covered like the one she'd seen outside Ethan's window.

Jefferson shouted something as the tug of war continued. She couldn't stand here waiting for the police to come, but what could she do that wouldn't endanger Ethan? Then it dawned on her that if she could position herself directly behind the ladder, she could take the photo of the man standing there. Then perhaps get the other man as he descended. But her movements might alert them to her presence.

The faint sound of sirens decided things for her. While the man at the bottom yelled for his companion to hurry before the cops arrived, she snapped his photo with her phone with the flash off. The ladder shook as the other kidnapper came down. Eve crouched low and aimed her camera up, praying the photos would be usable despite the leaves and the rain—and her shaking hands. She snapped as many photos as she could manage while praying the man hadn't gotten Ethan out the window.

"Why didn't you get the kid?"

"The dad wouldn't let go. Come on. The cops will be here soon."

The two men took off at a run toward the barn sitting toward the back of the property, leaving the ladder in place. Eve made her way back to the stoop and hauled herself up. She ignored her damp hair, only wanting to see with her own eyes Ethan was okay. This must be how mothers felt every single day of their child's life—this overwhelming need to keep their child safe and secure from the big bad world. One part of her recognized that most moms didn't have to contend with successive kidnapping attempts, but the emotions were the same.

She'd made it to the base of the stairs when someone pounded on the front door. "Police!"

Despite a burning desire to see Ethan, she detoured to the door. A pair of officers stood outside, blue lights flashing on the two patrol cars parked at the curb. "The two men who tried to grab Ethan fled toward the barn and woods at the back of the house. I need to check on my son upstairs."

She left the door open, assuming one of the officers would check the back, and rushed toward the stairs. When Jefferson appeared on the stair landing, Ethan in his arms, she took the steps two at a time to fling her arms around the two most important people in her life. Jefferson grunted as her weight collided with his body, but he accepted her hug without pulling away.

Ethan twisted until one of his arms went around her neck. She buried her face in Jefferson's shoulder and her son's chest, fighting back sobs of relief and fury.

"He's safe. It's okay." Jefferson's reassurances did little to calm her still-racing heart.

"He could have been…" She couldn't finish the thought, her body shaking with delayed shock.

"Mr. Smith, Dr. Davenport." The calm voice of Detective Janice Cunningham pulled Eve back to the present.

Eve extracted herself from the embrace she'd instigated and turned, swiping away moisture from her cheeks. "Let's go to the kitchen. I need more coffee."

"And I'm hungry. Fighting off bad men makes you want pancakes." Ethan's pronouncement diffused some of the tension.

"I'm not sure we have time for pancakes before the bus comes." By the expression on Jefferson's face, he wasn't sure about sending Ethan to school today, so Eve volunteered to make pancakes.

"You can tell Detective Cunningham about the bad man while I whip up the batter." She led the way into the kitchen, starting a third pot of coffee before using some paper towels to dry her hair. Then she hunted down the ingredients for pancakes. Jefferson plugged in an electric griddle before taking a seat to Ethan's right. As she measured and whisked the eggs, flour, sugar, oil, baking powder, milk, and salt together, she listened to Ethan's tale.

"I woke up because I smelled rain, which was funny because I didn't think it was supposed to rain today." Ethan slurped orange juice from a glass, clearly enjoying being the center of attention now that he was safe from harm.

Cunningham sat at the table across from Ethan, while

another officer had pulled in one of the dining room chairs and had taken a seat with his notebook out.

"I don't think it was," agreed the detective, her voice conversational. She seemed content to let Ethan talk with minimal questions.

"Then I saw the scary man with his face covered." Ethan gestured toward his mouth and nose, "and his hood pulled up over his head coming through the window. That's when I screamed."

Eve tested the griddle to see if it was hot enough, then ladeled the first six pancakes on the hot surface.

"I knew Dad would come." Ethan gave Jefferson a look so filled with adoration and certainty, it brought tears to Eve's eyes. If she'd had any doubts about how close the two were, that glance erased them, but it created doubt in her own heart about whether she should rock the boat by insisting on being part of Ethan's life. Jefferson and Ethan had weathered so much with George's death, she was unsure whether the introduction of a long-lost mother would be a positive thing for her son or would simply be too much for the young boy to handle.

"And he did," Ethan continued. "The man grabbed me, but Dad got hold of my legs and wouldn't let the bad man take me."

As Ethan relayed the tug of war between Jefferson and the bad man, Eve flipped the pancakes, then found the plates. She handed silverware to Ethan and Jefferson, but the detective said no thanks to pancakes. Cunningham asked Jefferson for his version of events while Eve served the hotcakes with butter and syrup to father and son before pouring more onto the griddle.

"Ma'am." An officer, his uniform wet from the rain, stood in the doorway. Cunningham excused herself, and the two retreated to the foyer, out of earshot from the kitchen. Eve finished cooking the rest of the pancakes, adding several more to Ethan's empty plate before placing two on a plate for herself.

She joined Ethan and Jefferson at the kitchen table with her breakfast and a fresh mug of coffee.

"Dad, do I hafta go to school today?" Ethan shoved in another bite of pancakes, then continued talking. "I've already missed the bus."

"No talking with food in your mouth," Jefferson admonished. "We'll talk about school once the police are finished here."

Eve listened to their banter while eating her own breakfast with an eye on the clock. 8:20. She texted Lily to let her know she would be late but would text again when she was on her way. Hopefully, Lily wouldn't have to reschedule too many appointments. She finished the last bite and washed it down with coffee. "I need to grab a change of clothes from my car."

Jefferson nodded, his attention on Ethan, who was trying to convince his dad he could indeed eat a fifth pancake.

"Thanks." After dumping her plate and mug in the sink, she wove her way through the officers and forensics team milling about the house. As she'd hoped, her duffel bag in the trunk held several changes of clothing. She brought the entire bag into the house, slipping into the guest room to check on Willoughby. The cat meowed his unhappiness at being stuck in the room with all the comings and goings outside.

"I hear you," she told him as she headed out. "I'll see if Ethan can visit you soon."

When Eve came out of her room, Cunningham motioned for her to join her in the living room. "I'd like to get your statement now, Dr. Davenport."

"Certainly." Eve walked her through her movements, then smacked her leg. "I completely forgot I took their pictures."

"You did what?"

Eve explained her hiding place, then opened her photo

app and handed her phone to the detective. "I hope they're usable, given the foliage of the bush."

Cunninham scrolled through them, then handed the phone back to Eve. "Our tech guys might be able to get sharper images. Send them to me." She rattled off her number, and Eve sent the pics.

"Did you find anything out back?" Eve prayed they had something useful to go on to find the men after Ethan.

"Some footprints and tire tracks where they'd parked a vehicle off a back road. Forensics are still going over the yard and ladder, so perhaps something else will be found too." Cunningham stood. "Your photos will help as well."

"Do you think it's safe for me to go to work today and Ethan to school?" Eve couldn't suppress the shiver at the memory of the man attacking her at the clinic.

"I will have an officer stationed outside the clinic."

"Like there was one outside Jefferson's house?"

The detective winced. "Someone called in a burglary attempt two streets over, so he left to respond to that call."

"Let me guess—false alarm." Eve threw up her hands in frustration. "Someone is targeting Ethan and me, and the only thing the police are doing is providing a cop to sit outside, which doesn't do any good if he leaves exactly when we needed assistance."

"I get that you're upset. I would be too, but we're doing the best we can." Cunningham's mild response made Eve ashamed at her harsh words.

"I know. I'm scared for Ethan and that the next kidnapping attempt will succeed." She blinked back tears. "Any news on the fire at my house?"

"I'm not in charge of that case, so I don't have any updates. However, Detective Feingold mentioned your uncle as a potential suspect, so we are following up with the Boston police."

"Thank you." Eve offered the detective a half smile. They

were doing their best, but she still worried about the repeated attempts to snatch Ethan. The attack on herself and the fire at her house paled in comparison to her son's safety. "I'd better get ready for work."

She left the detective and slipped back into the guest room, her nerves jangly and her emotions teetertottering from relief this latest attempt had been stymied to anger that no progress had been made in finding out why someone was after her and Ethan. As she showered, one thought repeated itself over and over in her mind—that Ethan's connection to her was the reason for the attempted kidnappings. That meant it had to be someone who knew Ethan was her son, a fact she only recently discovered herself. All that pointed to her uncle. Toweling off, she considered the flaw in that reasoning. If her uncle had wanted her dead, he could have done that anytime in her childhood, so the attacks on her now made no sense.

Unless something had happened recently to trigger the assaults. A headache intensified behind her eyes. Downing a couple of ibuprofen, she determined to dig deeper into her past to find the answers she was certain must lurk there.

CHAPTER

TEN

Jefferson handed Ethan a piece of sandpaper. "Rub it like this on the wood to smooth off those rough edges." He demonstrated, then let Ethan attempt it on his own.

His son's tongue stuck out between his lips as he concentrated on duplicating Jefferson's motion. The sandpaper slipped several times before Ethan managed to get into the rhythm. "I'm doing it!"

"Keep at it. You need to do all four legs."

"Okay." Ethan returned his attention to the straight pieces of wood Jefferson would attach to the base of a chair.

Jefferson enjoyed working with his hands, much preferring it to office work. When he'd needed to move back home to help with Ethan, he'd continued his studies in business, but on a whim had signed up for a woodworking class at the community college. To his surprise, he'd loved it, then had snagged an apprenticeship with an Amish furniture maker in Pennsylvania after graduating. By that time, George had a steady job as a beat cop in the Boston PD and Ethan was old enough for preschool, leaving Jefferson free to pursue his own calling.

A few years later, Jefferson had begun branching out on

his own, making a modest name for himself in handmade home furnishings. By the time of George's death, he had a business plan for his own furniture business. That gave him the flexibility to move Ethan down to Virginia and away from so many memories of George. Jefferson thought the change would be good for the both of them, but with the attempted kidnappings, he should have stayed in Boston.

His phone buzzed, and Eve's name and number flashed on the screen. He had resisted calling her all day, having decided to keep Ethan home from school while she went to work. Ethan had been delighted to play with Willoughby and help Jefferson in the shop, and his son hadn't mentioned the morning's incident at all.

"Aren't you gonna answer your phone?" Ethan snatched the device before Jefferson could snag it. "Dr. Eve is calling!" His son swiped to answer. "Hi, Dr. Eve. It's Ethan. Dad let me stay home from school today."

"Did he now?"

Jefferson could clearly hear Eve's voice as Ethan held the phone a few inches from his ear.

"What have you been up to?"

"He's letting me help him sand some furniture." Ethan scrunched up his face. "But he only let me watch one episode of *Teen Titans*."

"Wise man. Is he around?"

"Dad, she wants to talk to you." Ethan thrust the phone into Jefferson's hand before picking up the sandpaper.

"Stay in the barn," Jefferson reminded him.

"I only have a minute, but I heard from the fire marshal."

Jefferson's gut twisted as Eve related the findings of arson. He took a few steps away from Ethan and lowered his voice, his eyes still on his son. "Do they have any clues who did it?"

"None that they shared with me. What about the police?"

"Same. They were here until after lunch collecting

evidence." He rested his hips against a work bench. "How bad is the damage to your house?"

"Extensive." She spoke something he assumed to someone else. "Sorry about that. I'm not going to be able to move back home for a while, which brings me to why I'm calling. May I stay at your place a few more days until I figure out a permanent solution?"

He'd been expecting her request, and his traitorous heart leapt in his chest at the thought of seeing Eve more. He needed to quash those thoughts immediately—he wasn't even sure he could co-parent Ethan, so why would he think they could rekindle their high school relationship so easily? *Because you never stopped loving her.* He ignored that voice. "That's fine, but you know you don't have to find somewhere else."

Ack, why had he gone and done that?

"That's kind of you, but it's probably not a good idea for me to stay at your house on a long-term basis."

He shouldn't be disappointed at her dismissive tone, but he was, as if seeing him more often was of no particular interest to her. *You could change her mind.* No, and he wouldn't even try.

"Regardless, it's nothing you have to decide right away."

Ethan's head popped up. "Dad, ask her about dinner."

Right. The idea Ethan had had and Jefferson had supported, since it seemed to take his son's mind off the man who'd tried to grab him. "Ethan wanted to know if you'll be home for dinner."

"I'd planned to work late to catch up on the forms." The wistfulness in her tone contrasted with the previous coolness.

Time to play the kid card. "He's cooking his specialty and wanted to share it with his favorite doctor."

As he'd suspected, she caved. "All right, what time should I be there?"

"Six on the dot."

"See you then." She disconnected.

"You like her, don't you?"

Jefferson's gaze collided with his son's. "I do. She's nice."

Ethan rolled his eyes. "She's more than nice. You like her, like her."

Heat warmed the back of his neck. "Of course I like her. You like her too."

"Daaaaddd, stop being so obstinate."

Jefferson hid a smile behind his hand at the big word. "Where'd you learn the word obstinate?"

"School. I've seen the way you look at her."

Oh, no. Had his former feelings somehow become apparent to Ethan—and Eve? "How do I look at her?"

"Like she's your favorite ice cream flavor." Ethan shook out his hand. "I'm tired of sanding and my hand hurts."

Jefferson checked the time. "Let's clean up and get started on dinner." While Ethan helped him sweep and put away tools, his son's words reverberated throughout his mind— Ethan knew how much Jefferson liked coconut chocolate chip ice cream and now he knew how much Jefferson liked Eve.

EVE LAID THE PAPER NAPKIN ON HER LAP TO WAIT FOR ETHAN TO bring in the main course, which he had prepared "with my own two hands. Dad only supervised me."

"Bacon-wrapped hot dogs with cheese!" Ethan announced as he carefully placed the platter with his culinary offering on the table. "We have french fries and baked beans too."

"Smells delicious." Eve blinked back sudden tears as a memory of Jefferson and George's mother delivering a tray with similar hot dogs during one of the Wednesday night meals Eve enjoyed. All during high school, she had become a staple at the Smith dinner table that one evening a week. It had been her uncle's standing poker night, and he had allowed her to escape from the cold atmosphere of dinner with him and Lorraine to be part of a real family.

"Don't forget the ketchup." Jefferson set a bowl with crinkle cut fries on the table alongside the baked beans.

"Got it!" Ethan raced back into the kitchen and came out seconds later with the condiment. "Can I pray tonight?"

"Sure," Jefferson said. He threw Eve an apologetic glance. "We hold hands to say grace."

"Okay." She accepted Ethan's hand with a grin in his direction but avoided eye contact with Jefferson as he encased her hand in his. She closed her eyes but couldn't concentrate on the blessing because of the memories crowding her mind of other times Jefferson had held her hand. In the hallways at school. Watching a movie at the AMC theater. Before Wednesday dinner at his parents' home. During one of their many walks around Boston's Public Garden, the nation's first public botanical garden.

Ethan squeezed her hand and let go, jolting Eve back to the present. She removed her hand from Jefferson's and reached for the tongs. "I can't wait to try your rapper dogs."

Ethan's eyes widened. "How'd you know that's what we call them?"

She placed one of the hot dogs on her plate. "I remember Jefferson's mom serving these when I used to eat dinner with them."

Ethan scooped a big pile of french fries onto his plate. "I forgot you knew my two dads when you were little."

"Not as little as you, but yes, I did know Jefferson and George quite well." She added a spoonful of baked beans, then some fries to her plate. Using her knife, she cut off a bite of hot dog, then forked it into her mouth. "Umm, just as good as Mrs. Smith's."

"Really? I'll have to tell Granny that the next time I talk to her." Ethan shoved a handful of fries into his mouth.

"Do you see your parents often?" She dipped a fry into some ketchup on her plate.

"Not as much as they would like." Jefferson drank from his water glass. "They were not happy with our move to Twin Oaks, but I—we—needed a change of scenery. Why did you choose Twin Oaks to practice medicine?"

"It's a far cry from my girlhood dreams of running a prestigious cancer research center, isn't it?" She laughed at her youthful ideas, ones she recalled sharing with Jefferson during their senior year. "I had to do a rotation on a pediatric ward early in medical school, and I was hooked. Switched my focus from research to pediatrics the next semester. As for Twin Oaks, I didn't want to cater to only those who could afford healthcare. With all the farms and orchards in the Shenandoah Valley, there is a big migrant community. I take part in a free mobile clinic that visits the farms during the harvest."

"How is the mobile clinic funded?"

Jefferson seemed genuinely interested in her philanthropic work, so Eve outlined the ways they raised money for the clinic—business donations and an annual Apple Blossoms Dance to coincide with the last day of the town's Apple Blossom Festival, held the second weekend in September.

"Aw, we missed it." Ethan reached for the french fry bowl, but Jefferson moved it away.

"I think you've had enough fries for one meal."

The boy's shoulders slumped.

"But remember, we do have dessert." Jefferson winked at Ethan, who brightened immediately.

"That's right! Can we have it now?"

Jefferson looked at Eve, who shrugged. "Now's a good a time as any, but I'm surprised you can fit more food in your tummy. You ate two hot dogs and mountain of french fries."

Ethan giggled. "It wasn't a mountain of fries."

"No?" Eve cocked her head. "Are you sure? Looked like a mountain to me."

Jefferson cleared the table while Ethan kept insisting he hadn't eaten that many fries and Eve teasing him about the large amount he had consumed. Her phone buzzed, and she reflexively checked it. The office service number, meaning the call was being routed from the practice. "I'm on call tonight, so I'd better get this."

She rose and moved into the living room for privacy. "Dr. Davenport."

"I'm not sure why you had to change your last name."

Eve sank onto the sofa, her heart jackhammering at the sound of her uncle's voice. She started to form an answer to his implied criticism but stopped herself. She didn't have to please him because he had no control over her life any longer. "Why are you calling?"

"Can't a man call his favorite niece to see how she's doing?"

"You've never done so before." She fisted her hand, then relaxed it a finger at a time to slow her heart rate.

"Maybe if you'd shared your new address and phone number with me, I would have contacted you sooner."

She held her breath, letting it out slowly to a count of five. Ronan certainly knew which buttons to push, but she wasn't a child cowed by his actions. Maybe a switch in topics would remind him of why he called. She could simply hang up, but with her uncle, it was better to know the why behind his actions sooner rather than later. "How's Lorraine?"

"Your aunt is doing fine, off at her book club this evening."

"Good for her." She waited while the silence built between them like a bricklayer building a wall.

Then Ronan cleared his throat. "So you moved to Virginia."

Since he hadn't asked a question, she didn't respond.

"That's not too far from Boston."

This time, she decided to end the conversation that appeared to be heading nowhere. "I've got to go."

"Before you do, I did need to talk to you about something."

Her heart rate quickened at his forced casual tone.

"With your twenty-fifth birthday coming up, there are some papers that need your signature."

No way was she going to Boston to sign papers, but her curiosity was piqued. "What kind of papers?"

"Nothing too exciting, but they need your John Hancock before next Thursday."

Eve couldn't recall signing anything when she turned eighteen or twenty-one and couldn't think of any reason she would need to sign papers now, but she did have a solution to propose. "You can send any papers to my attorney David Keene. I'll email you his address."

"No need to get lawyers involved." The jovial tone of her uncle didn't fool her for a minute.

"I'm not coming to Boston. If you want me to look at the papers, you'll need to send them to Mr. Keene."

"Maybe Lorraine and I will take a little trip south to see our favorite niece and bring the papers then."

"Suit yourself. I've got to run. Bye." It took her two tries to hit the disconnect button.

"You okay?"

Eve squealed at Jefferson's question, dropping her phone to the carpet. "You startled me."

"Didn't mean too." He crossed to her and picked up her phone. "You're trembling."

Her body shuddered as if to confirm his words. "My uncle called."

"Donahue?" He held out the phone to her.

She nodded, then took it, slipping it directly into her back pocket, unsure if her fingers would be able to hold onto the device.

"What did he want?" As if anticipating her next question, he added, "Ethan's taking his bath."

"He wanted me to sign some papers before I turn twenty-five next week."

"What papers?"

"Exactly the question I asked him but one he didn't answer. I told him to send them to my attorney David Keene."

"You have a lawyer on retainer?"

"Not exactly. David's a friend who helped me buy into the practice." She rubbed her arms to ward off the chill that had settled over her during the call. "My uncle has never asked me to sign papers before."

"I think you did the right thing, asking him to send them to the attorney."

"Dad! I'm ready to get out!"

"I'd better go or he's liable to swamp the entire bathroom." Jefferson bounded up the stairs, leaving Eve alone with her thoughts.

And her fears. Because while she'd shared a few things with Jefferson about her uncle's controlling ways, she hadn't shared her biggest one—that Ronan had somehow engineered the death of her parents for the insurance money, which meant he was capable of trying to eliminate her and Ethan.

CHAPTER

ELEVEN

Jefferson smothered a yawn as he pulled on jeans and a sweatshirt. Ethan snoozed on, unusual for a Saturday morning when he frequently awoke with the birds. Maybe the gray, drizzly spring day contributed to his sleeping in past seven. Whatever the case, Jefferson would treasure the few minutes of solitude. He'd heard Eve leave half an hour ago for her rotation at the mobile clinic, which drove out to where the migrant workers were picking apples or harvesting other produce at the multiple farms dotting the fertile Shenandoah Valley.

He missed her.

After less than forty-eight hours, he'd gotten used to having Eve in his home. Her boots lined up next to his and Ethan's by the side mudroom door. Her sweater draped over the back of a kitchen chair.

He missed her with an ache that echoed the hurt when he'd broken up with her the day before their senior prom. Then he'd convinced himself he was doing the right thing, the noble thing, setting his beautiful little bird free. He'd known she would never agree to dating other people in the fall when they both went away to different colleges. But since she was two years his junior, book smart but naïve in the ways of the world, he'd come to the painful conclusion that breaking up was the only way for her to truly be free to find out if the love she felt for him was one that could go the distance.

Jefferson had been convinced his was, and from the warm feelings in his heart toward the woman she'd become, he still loved her. Not that he had any intention of acting on that emotion, not with Ethan's life in danger and uncertainty about how to incorporate Eve into their lives without harming Ethan's memories of his biological father.

He poured coffee into the Best Dad Ever mug Ethan had given George last Christmas, his mind drifting back to the car accident that had taken George's life. Ethan might have been killed as well, had he not gotten sick and stayed home with Jefferson while George went to drop off the gift for one of Ethan's classmates. Ethan had tried to convince his father he wasn't too sick to attend the party at a local trampoline park, but his flushed cheeks told a different story. George said he had to stop by work for a few minutes and could bring the gift to the birthday boy on his way. He never made it to the party.

After deciding to push off breakfast until Ethan got up, Jefferson settled at the kitchen table with his laptop. Eve's insistence that her uncle could be behind the attacks gnawed at him. The why made no sense, but the timing of Donahue's call about signing papers before she turned twenty-five contributed to his unease. Perhaps a little internet sleuthing into Eve's background might shed some light on the murki- ness. She'd left a yellow legal pad on the kitchen table with her notes, so he'd see where she'd left off. Since it was Ethan's family too, he quelled the twinge of conscience telling him he should ask her permission first.

He hit a roadblock with her parents almost immediately. Lack of basic info about her mother and father, such as where they had been married, made it difficult to go beyond the few newspaper articles about the auto accident in Indiana that had claimed their lives. He quickly discovered neither parent had been born in Indiana nor had the couple married there, according to the Indiana Department of Health Division of Vital Records website. While he found their death certificates listing injuries from a car accident as the cause for both, he could find no other information. Maybe his mom would remember where they had been from. He sent her a text and was amused with her fast reply—Arizona—and a request for a visit from her favorite grandson soon. He promised to firm up plans for a trip in a few months, then went on the Arizona Bureau of Vital Records website. However, because he wasn't related, he didn't have the necessary documents to get a copy of Ethan's other grandparents' birth certificates.

Back to Google, which turned out to be his friend with an announcement of the marriage of Maeve and Nigel Brandt in the *Phoenix Gazette*. The photo accompanying the piece took his breath away. Eve was the spitting image of her mother. No doubt these were her parents. He plugged in Nigel's name into the paper's search engine, expecting to find only archived articles but instead a more recent story popped up first.

Owen Brandt Dead at Age 93

Sedona, Ariz.—Owen Brandt III, the 93-year-old scion of Trigon Precision, died on March 22 at his Sedona ranch. Brandt took the manufacturing company of automobile and airplane parts his namesake grandfather started in 1908 from a small business to a multi-billion-dollar international corporation. It was Brandt, after returning from World War II, who added the lucrative airplane parts division before most manufacturers had even considered the possibilities of expanded air travel.

Jefferson skimmed to the end of the article, which detailed Eve's grandfather's extensive life, to read the list of descendants, expecting to find Eve's name among the grandchildren. But it wasn't there. He re-read it more closely. Owen had had three children with his first wife, Evelyn, who had died before Eve had been born. With his second wife, Charlene, Brandt had another four children. The very end of the list of heirs had the word "predeceased" in front of Eve's father's, mother's, and then her own name. According to the Brandt family, all members of Nigel Brandt's family were dead. Very strange since surely Ronan Donahue would have informed them Eve had survived the car accident that killed his sister. Why would he have hidden Eve's existence from her father's family? He added a note below her beautiful penmanship to contact the company on Monday to find out which law firm represented the estate.

"Hey, Dad. Whatcha doing?" Ethan leaned over Jefferson's shoulder.

"Looking into something." Jefferson closed the computer as his stomach rumbled. "How about you help me whip up some scrambled eggs?"

"Not hungry."

Jefferson peered closer at Ethan, noting the flushed cheeks and lethargy in his usually bouncy child. "Why not?"

Ethan swiped the corner of his mouth. "My tongue feels funny and my tummy hurts."

Before Jefferson could ask a follow up question, Ethan's eyes widened and he bolted. Jefferson hustled after him, wincing at the sound of retching in the hall bathroom. He paused in the doorway to see Ethan hugging the toilet.

"You okay, buddy?" Worry nibbled at him, as Ethan generally had an iron constitution, as Mom put it. The boy hardly ever got the stomach bug, even when it ran through his class at school. He crouched beside him and rubbed Ethan's back while his son vomited again.

"Dad?" The fear in Ethan's voice ratcheted up his concern. "Why is everything blurry?"

"I don't know." He got his phone and started to punch in 911, then paused. Eve might be able to provide more targeted guidance. He pulled up her contact info and hit the call button. "But I'm calling Dr. Eve."

"Good." Ethan slumped into Jefferson.

The phone rang several times without an answer. Jefferson was ready to disconnect and call 911 when Eve answered. "Hey, Jefferson. I can't talk—"

"Ethan's sick. He threw up, but said his vision is blurry and his tongue felt funny. I think it's more than a stomach bug."

"I need to see him." She hung up, but immediately his phone vibrated with an incoming video call from Eve.

He swiped to answer. "Here he is." He turned the camera toward Ethan, who lay against him.

"Hey, Ethan. Can you open your eyes for me?"

No response to Eve's question. Jefferson jostled his son, and Ethan opened his eyes.

"You don't look like you're feeling well," Eve said.

Ethan blinked rapidly. "You're all out of focus."

"I bet I am. Can you open your mouth real wide for me?"

Ethan complied, and Jefferson noted his puffy tongue. Eve thanked him, then said, "The hospital in Staunton's too far away, so I'll meet you at the Twin Oaks Clinic."

Alarm flared through him at her words. "You—"

"Hurry, Jefferson." Her voice caught. "I think he's having an extreme allergic reaction."

Eve apologized to her nurse, saying a family emergency needed her immediate attention. Thank goodness they had already tackled the most critical cases at the migrant mobile clinic. Her capable nurse practitioner could easily handle the remaining workers and their children. She raced for her SUV and tore out of the farm's gravel parking lot as fast as she could. *Please let Ethan be okay, God. Please. I can't lose him after finding him again.*

She requested Siri to call the clinic, identifying herself to the receptionist and asking to speak to the doctor.

"Dr. Appleton."

"It's Eve, James." She rapidly laid out her suspicion that Ethan was having an allergic reaction.

"Could be poison too," Appleton responded when she paused to draw in a breath.

Her heart constricted at the thought someone had deliberately harmed her child. "I'm about half an hour away, but Jefferson is bringing Ethan in now. Once you see him, you'll be better able to decide whether to treat to an allergic reaction or poison ingestion."

"Don't worry—we'll take good care of him."

Eve disconnected as she braked at an all-way stop, then asked Siri to connect her to Detective Cunningham. While she waited for the call to go through, she tapped her fingers on the steering wheel as an eighteen-wheeler made a right-hand turn. Her turn came, and she hit the gas, a prayer on her lips as the call rolled to voicemail.

"Detective Cunningham, it's Dr. Davenport." Eve negotiated a hairpin turn at speed, ignoring the yellow signs to slow down. "Jefferson is taking Ethan to the Twin Oaks Clinic with a possible allergic reaction or poisoning. I'm on my way to meet him there."

She ended the call, only to have her phone ring immediately with the detective calling her back, too fast to have listened to her voicemail. Eve answered and repeated her message. "We don't know what Ethan ingested or came in contact with. The clinic doctor mentioned it could be poison and not an allergic reaction."

"I'll have an officer swing by the clinic to get the house key and meet him at the Smiths to do a sweep."

"Thank you." Eve whipped the vehicle into the parking

lot of the clinic, which sat on the western end of the town. Jefferson had parked his car in a handicapped spot near the entrance. She grabbed her phone and rushed inside.

The receptionist waved her through to the back. "They arrived about five minutes ago."

Eve pushed through the swinging doors. A nurse pointed to cubicle three, and she yanked back the curtain to see Dr. Appleton bending over a pale Ethan. Jefferson clutched the boy's hand on the opposite side of the bed.

"How is he?" She touched Ethan's sock foot, unable to stop herself.

"He's swallowed his first dose of the activated charcoal, and we've started the IV drip." Dr. Appleton straightened, giving her a full-face glimpse of her son, who lay still with his eyes closed.

She gasped as the doctor's words confirmed he thought Ethan had been poisoned.

"Any ideas as to what he might have taken?" Dr. Appleton asked.

Jefferson shook his head. "The police are checking the house."

"How could anyone get to him?" They had been so careful. "You were with him all day yesterday."

Jefferson rubbed a hand over his beard. "I have no idea. Ethan's not the kind of kid to eat anything dubious."

"We'll keep an eye on his condition and administer more activated charcoal pills as necessary until we have more info on the type of poison." The doctor glanced from Jefferson to Eve. "I'll be back to check on him, but don't hesitate to call if you notice any changes in his condition."

Eve thanked him and moved to the other side of the bed, standing across from Jefferson. Tears pressed hotly against the backs of her eyes, but she refused to let them fall. Ethan needed her to be strong, not weak. Her phone buzzed, and she glanced at the incoming call from the detective. "Did you find something?"

"There was what looks like crumbs of chocolate on the bedside table in Ethan's room. I'm texting you a photo and gathering them for analysis," Cunningham said.

"Bring it to the clinic," Eve instructed. "We have a small lab in the back that I can use to determine what was in the chocolate."

"Will be there shortly."

Eve's phone vibrated with the text from the detective showing the chocolate crumbles. "Did Ethan eat chocolate last night?" She showed him the photo.

Jefferson frowned. "No, we don't have any chocolate in the house."

"You left a bar on my pillow." Ethan's weak voice startled Eve, who had thought the boy asleep.

"I—" Jefferson started to answer, but Eve grabbed his hand and shook her head. She didn't want Ethan upset thinking he'd done the wrong thing, not when he was so sick.

"What did the candy look like?" She kept her tone conversational, as if his answer didn't matter.

"I'm really tired." Ethan yawned. "I don't wanna talk anymore."

Eve motioned to Jefferson to step outside the cubicle so they could talk privately. She didn't want to chance Ethan overhearing them and becoming frightened.

"How serious is this?" Jefferson's question echoed her own thoughts.

"Until we know what he ingested, I can't say. But it's not too fast-acting, which is good news." She glanced back at the still child, her mind ticking through the list of possible poisons. "His symptoms aren't consistent with an overdose of fentanyl."

"Fentanyl!" Jefferson's outburst drew the attention of a passing nurse.

Eve laid a hand on his arm. "I said it's not fentanyl." If it had been, Ethan would likely be dead by now, but she wouldn't tell his worried father that. "I'm trying to think of what poison it could be, but until we know for sure, the activated charcoal and the IV fluids should keep him safe."

"Shouldn't they pump his stomach or something?"

"If he's already vomited, then there's no reason to subject him to that." She'd had to pump several stomachs during her residency and never wanted to repeat that unpleasant yet life-saving task.

"Dr. Davenport?" A nurse held an evidence bag. "Detective Cunningham said you need this right away."

She accepted the bag, then said to Jefferson, "I'm going to see if I can identify the poison in the clinic's lab. Send someone to get me if Ethan's condition changes."

She turned to go, but Jefferson grabbed her arm. Before she could react, he'd crushed her into his arms, wrapping her in a cocoon of warmth. She slipped her arms around his waist and laid her head on his strong shoulder, allowing herself a few seconds of shared comfort. "He'll be okay."

"I pray so." He released her. "Now go find out who poisoned our son."

With a crisp nod, she spun on her heel and darted toward the lab at the back of the clinic. His words "our son" echoed in her mind, giving her hope that one day, she might be able to fully acknowledge Ethan as her son and be part of his life, not as his doctor but as his mother.

CHAPTER

TWELVE

E ve straightened, annoyed and puzzled that the usual suspects of household poisons— antidepressants, antihistamines, cardiovascular drugs, painkillers, sedatives, stimulants, and vitamins/supplements—had been ruled out as being in the chocolate Ethan had consumed. She'd run out of ideas of things to search for, and the sample size had diminished to the point where she needed direction in order not to waste it. Maybe a close look under the microscope might give her a clue as to what had been mixed with the chocolate.

She rolled her shoulders to ease the tension building there from bending over the samples during the four hours she'd been in the lab. Jefferson had been sending regular text updates on Ethan's condition, which hadn't worsened. Unfortunately, it hadn't gotten better either, but she wasn't going to stop searching for what was making him sick until she found the answer. *Please God, help me! We need to know how to treat Ethan so he'll get better.*

Her phone buzzed, interrupting her prayer.

Dr. says Ethan's heartbeat is becoming more irregular.

Her own heart jumped in response to Jefferson's text about a new symptom.

How irregular?

Enough that he wants to give him a beta-blocker.

Then the heartbeat wasn't smoothing out but staying irregular. Not a good sign at all because it could mean the poison was starting to affect some of his organs. She wouldn't share that with Jefferson. No need to pile on more worry for his son.

That should help regulate the heartbeat.

Have you ID'd the poison?

Not yet. It's not one of the usual suspects, but I'm going to look at it under a microscope and hopefully find some clues for what to test for next.

Keep me posted.

Before creating a slide for the microscope with a portion of the remaining chocolate crumbs, she added the new symptom of irregular heartbeat to the list of others compiled with Jefferson's help: blurry vision, nausea/vomiting, lethargy, no appetite, swollen tongue. She'd tried entering the list into a poison database, but the results were too numerous to be of any help. With tweezers, she pinched a few crumbs onto a glass slide and placed it under the microscope. At first, all she saw were the chocolate molecules, but then she noted something green and white mixed with the brown.

Increasing magnification brought the green-and-white flakes into crisper view, allowing her to see more clearly their molecular structure. A line of distinct vascular bundles ran through the green fleck, while the white one showed a series of tiny folds and a pollen grain. She readjusted the microscope and peered again at the slide before concluding she hadn't been mistaken. The chocolate contained a plant leaf and flower, but which one?

Google would probably give her the top choices, so she opened a new search and keyed in "Flowering plants harmful to humans." As she scrolled through results, she glanced at each picture to see if she'd spotted them near the Smith house, fully aware that the plant could have been from anywhere. However, her gut screamed the poisoning was opportunity coupled with proximity, and that the plant would be something Jefferson had in his yard.

She dismissed the first three—oleander, deadly night-shade, and water hemlock—because those definitely hadn't been visible around his house. The fourth one made her pause. Lily of the valley. She'd removed a potted lily of the valley from her room at Jefferson's house to the back stoop because of the plant's toxicity to cats but hadn't realized it could poison humans too. Eve hit call under Cunningham's name while she read the signs of lily of the valley poisoning. All of them aligned with Ethan's symptoms.

"Detective Cunningham."

"It's Dr. Davenport."

"How's Ethan?"

"Not any better, but I'm calling because I think I know what might have been mixed with the chocolate. Do you know if there was a potted plant—lily of the valley—sitting on the back stoop?"

"Let me scroll through the photos we took while investigating the attempted kidnapping."

Eve waited while she checked on the treatment if someone consumed the flower. It appeared they were doing all they could and that Ethan should recover in a few days, if she was correct about the source.

"No, there was no potted plant anywhere in the backyard."

"Then I think someone took it and mixed it with chocolate to poison Ethan. I'm going to get a sample of Ethan's blood and test it for convallotoxin to be sure."

"Will he be okay?"

"He should be as we treat the symptoms." Eve prayed she was right.

"Any idea how he got the chocolate?"

"Ethan mentioned something about a chocolate bar being left on his pillow that he thought came from his father, but that's about all we've been able to get from him."

"I'll send someone over for the rest of the chocolate crumbs. If you can get a vial of blood from him for our labs, we'll also test it to build our case since we both know Ethan didn't chop up the plant and mix it with chocolate."

"Right, thanks. I'll have the samples boxed and waiting at reception for you within the hour."

"Let me know how the little guy's doing."

Eve disconnected the call, then gathered the remaining chocolate bits and placed them back into the original evidence envelope the detective had given her before printing out the results from the tests she'd conducted. Then she labeled two vials with Ethan's info and left the lab.

After checking in at the nurse's station and alerting them to her mission, Eve eased into Ethan's cubicle without announcing herself. Jefferson slouched in a chair beside the bed with his eyes closed and his hand holding his son's. Ethan lay sleeping, his brown hair the only bit of color against the white sheets and blanket. She hated to wake Jefferson and Ethan, but she needed to do a blood draw in order to verify her suspicion about the source of the poison.

"Hey." She gently shook Jefferson's shoulder.

His eyes popped open, and he straightened.

"No change," she hastened to reassure him, noting the panic flaring in his eyes. "But can we talk outside for a minute?"

He scrubbed a hand over his beard. "Sure."

Eve moved a few steps away from the curtain, unsure if Ethan had awakened or not. She pitched her voice low. "I think I've discovered what poison was in the chocolate."

Quickly, she ran through her discovery. "I'll need to take some blood to confirm it."

"Lily of the valley?" Jefferson appeared to struggle to process the information. "My mom gave me that plant before we left Boston. Someone had given it to her, but with her two cats, she didn't want it in the house. I had no idea it was also poisonous to humans."

"I didn't either, but someone knew and took the plant I put on the back porch."

"It's not there?"

"I confirmed with the detective that it's gone." She recapped her conversation with Cunningham. "Now I need to draw blood to test it for convallotoxin and give the police a vial so they can conduct their own tests."

Dr. Appleton approached. "How's the patient?"

Eve brought him up to speed, adding that the current treatment should continue until Ethan's symptoms abated.

"I concur, but he'll need to be moved to a hospital, as we don't have beds for overnight accommodation," Dr. Appleton said. "I'll get one of the nurses to make arrangements for him to be transferred to Staunton Medical."

"But he'll be okay?" Jefferson's question echoed the one pulsing through Eve's heart.

Despite her medical knowledge, she too needed reassurance Ethan would recover.

"If Dr. Davenport's assessment that he ingested lily of the valley is correct, then he should make a full recovery." Dr. Appleton met Eve's gaze. "The medication seems to be regulating his heartbeat."

She picked up on what he wasn't saying—that Ethan might have to take the medicine to keep his heart beating properly for several months or even a lifetime—but that was a conversation they could have later, after the initial crisis passed and they had more information about his condition. Now she simply said, "Good. I'll get the blood drawn."

JEFFERSON CARRIED HIS TRAY OVER TO WHERE EVE SAT IN THE hospital cafeteria, nursing a cup of coffee and picking at a pastry. With her hair up in a messy bun and wearing jeans and t-shirt, she could have passed for a high schooler instead of a doctor. His heart pitter-pattered as memories of their senior year, when they had been inseparable, assailed him. Eve had always been serious, rarely smiling or joining in the other teenage antics of their classmates. Her mature demeanor belied her young years, having skipped two grades in elementary school to graduate at sixteen. Something about her had immediately drawn his attention when he and George had transferred in midway through their freshman year. When the chemistry teacher paired him and Eve for a class project, they had found much in common outside the classroom.

He slid his tray with a burger, fries, and milkshake onto the table. "That's not much of a lunch."

"Not that hungry. I did eat a yogurt and a banana." She pointed to the remains of a yogurt cup and banana peel on her tray. "I can't believe someone tried to kill Ethan with lily of the valley leaves and petals. Thank goodness they didn't realize the roots were more deadly or he…" Her voice choked off the last words.

He covered her hand with his. "The doctors say he will be make a full recovery, and he's more alert now that it's been more than twenty-four hours."

"But what if he'll need to take the beta-blockers the rest of his life to keep his heartbeat regular?"

"We don't know if that's going to happen." He squeezed her hand, wishing he could take away her worry about Ethan. The love she had for her son was evident to everyone, and he acknowledged it meant he needed to figure out a way to enfold her into Ethan's life once they caught whoever was behind the attacks.

She blotted her cheeks with a paper napkin. "I know. It's what I tell the parents of my patients all the time. It's the first time I've been on the other side."

He patted her hand before picking up a fry. "I wish I could say it gets easier, but it doesn't. There will always be something to worry about when you have a kid."

That brought a brief smile to her lips. "Thanks for not giving me false comfort."

"Anytime." He bit into his burger.

"I'm glad he's recovering."

"I gave the detective permission to thoroughly search the house to see if there was any other candy left behind."

"And?"

"Nothing, plus no sign of the plant around the yard. Whoever did this saw an opportunity and took it."

"It's troubling that they've moved from kidnapping to attempted murder with Ethan."

"I agree, and the Twin Oaks Police Department has promised round-the-clock protection." He popped a fry into his mouth and chewed. "Not bad for a hospital cafeteria."

"But not as good as the spicy fries you and George made in the air fryer."

He willingly detoured onto memory lane. "Do you recall the time you snuck in extra cayenne pepper?"

"Your dad took the first bite of the fries and turned beet red." Amusement danced in her eyes. "I thought I'd never be invited back to Wednesday dinners after that."

Jefferson caught the wistfulness behind the statement, the testament that those simple family meals had been so important to Eve. Now that he knew more of her upbringing, he wished he had been more understanding and not teased her so much about wanting to be part of his family. He couldn't change the past, but perhaps he could bring a little more light into her memories of it. "You know, my mom used to tell us if we didn't behave, she'd adopt you instead."

"Really?" Eve ducked her head. "I loved your mom. She was so welcoming, so real. She didn't ask me stuff about school like all the other adults. She talked to me as if I was a real person." She sighed. "I'm sure she hates me now."

While his father did have some choice words to say about Eve when Donahue had dropped off the baby so abruptly, Jefferson didn't recall his mother sharing her opinion. He thought back to the many conversations they'd had about Ethan and the way Eve had behaved and recalled his mom not joining in or changing the subject. "You know, I don't think she ever did."

"How could she not?"

The hurt behind those words tore at his heart. How could he have so easily believed the lies Donahue had said? Because his pride had been hurt by what he saw as her betrayal with George.

"What my uncle said about me was despicable. I'd hate me under those circumstances."

"I don't hate you, Eve." He hadn't meant to say it but recognized the truth. He had stopped hating her years ago, coming to a measure of forgiveness. Running into her again had reawakened some of those feelings but hearing her side of the story had completely erased any lingering seeds of anger. But she might feel anger toward him and George once she heard what he'd promised his brother to tell her. "There's something you need to know."

"I thought Ethan was doing better and would be discharged this afternoon." Anxiety flared in her face.

"Sorry, Ethan's fine, and yes, the doctor said he could go home once they do another blood check after lunch to make sure the poison's out of his system." He shoved the tray back, his appetite gone as his stomach knotted. This was not going to be an easy conversation. "Several years ago, George wasn't in a good place mentally. He'd been on the Boston PD as a beat cop for a few years but had started drinking after his shifts with his buddies. That morphed into continuing the alcohol consumption at home. It grew steadily worse until he was basically hung over at work every shift. How he managed to hold onto his job, I'll never know."

"I'm so sorry." The compassion in Eve's voice soothed him, but she wouldn't feel that way once she heard the rest of the story.

"One night, when I confronted him about his alcohol abuse, he blurted out the truth—that he had spiked your punch with alcohol and Ecstasy on prom night." He paused, unable to continue until he'd regained his composure. He'd loved his fraternal twin but had been so angry at hearing what George had done to sweet Eve.

Eve reared back, her brown eyes wide. "He drugged me?"

"Yes." No sense sugar coating the bald truth. "He'd always had a crush on you and had been envious of our relationship. That's why, when I broke up with you, he swooped in and asked you to prom."

"I only said yes to make you jealous. I mean, I liked George, but I wanted to go to prom with you."

"I know." He'd broken her heart, wanting the hurt to be over and done with before they parted ways in the fall. "I was stupid, sure I was doing the noble thing by letting you go. I didn't believe your love for me was strong enough to survive the distance, no matter what you promised."

Disbelief bracketed her mouth. "So you thought casting me aside would be better."

"Like I said, stupid." He had gone this far, he might as well go further. "I was so in love with you, I couldn't handle not knowing who you might be seeing. Jealousy is indeed a green-eyed monster, and it got hold of me hard that spring."

"So you lanced the wound." Her medical analogy fit.

"Better to have the pain when I was prepared for it than

waiting for the other shoe to drop." Talk about mixing his idioms, but he didn't bother fixing his grammar. Not when he needed her to hear the rest. "But that doesn't excuse my actions, and what followed. Because…" He swallowed, his mouth dry and his palms moist. He gulped the rest of his coffee. "Because I knew George had been running with a rougher crowd, drinking beer. He'd always been envious of our relationship, of me. School was easy for me, but not for him. I didn't learn until later how much he resented me for all of it."

Her eyes filled with tears. "And I was the means for his revenge."

"I think he saw a chance and took it. Spiked your drink to see what would happen."

She ran a finger around the edge of the tray. "He took advantage of me. I was barely aware of what was happening and kept confusing him with you. However, I do recall being a willing participant in the, er, bedroom activities, but again, I thought it was you." A tear slipped down her cheek. "Some part of me knew it was wrong, but I missed you so much, I, well, didn't protest too much."

He captured her hand with his. "I'm so sorry, Eve. George was too. Not long after I confronted him about his drinking, he started attending Alcoholics Anonymous. His sponsor introduced him to Jesus, and he began going to church and changing his ways. He stopped blaming you for dropping off Ethan like a sack of potatoes and started taking responsibility for his own actions."

More tears dampened her cheeks, and her fingers curled around his own.

Jefferson needed to tell her the rest. "George tried to find you. He wanted you to be involved in Ethan's life. He also wanted to apologize for his actions. I have a letter he wrote shortly before he died. He made me promise to find you one day and deliver the letter. I have it at the house."

"Okay." She sniffled. "He didn't hate me for giving up Ethan?"

"Not in the end." He drew in a breath, letting it out in a whoosh of air. "And I don't either."

Her eyes widened. "You don't?"

"I should have questioned things more back then, but I was young and stupid."

"I think we've firmly established how stupid you were as an eighteen-year-old." Her wry comment brought an answering smile to his lips.

"Good point. What I'm trying to say is, please forgive me for treating you so shabbily when we first met again."

"I would have been angry too."

"That doesn't let me off the hook."

Her shoulders squared as if a great weight had been lifted off. "Thank you. I accept your apology."

He moved around the table to sit in the chair next to hers. "Eve, you asked me if you could be part of Ethan's life. It was George's greatest wish that you would be part of his son's life. Once we have answers to who's been after you and Ethan and that person is caught, we can discuss what that will look like going forward."

"You mean it?" The hope shining in her eyes tugged at his heart.

"Yes, I do."

She flung herself into his arms. "Thank you, Jefferson."

He breathed in the scent of rosemary and sunshine, what he'd always associated with Eve. As he held her close, he thanked God for bringing them to this first healing step and prayed for additional time to fully bring closure to their past. If that meant creating a new opening for a future together, well, he was open to that too.

THIRTEEN

Eve waved to Ethan buckled into the backseat of Jefferson's car, then climbed into her vehicle for the drive back to Twin Oaks. Ethan's bloodwork indicated the poison was nearly gone, and the medication was keeping his heart rate steady. She prayed he would not have to take the medicine for long but only time would tell if the poison had damaged his heart permanently. She pulled out behind Jefferson for the ninety-minute trip, thankful she had the time to think about their earlier conversation in the hospital cafeteria. The news that George had slipped her a mickey initially shocked her, but as she mulled over the evening—and George's past behavior—it wasn't so surprising. Even while dating Jefferson, she'd known George had a crush on her. What she hadn't realized until later was how much he resented his twin brother, which explained the constant digs at Jefferson from George that he passed off as teasing. Their parents had attempted to curb George's cutting remarks, so George tempered his remarks in their presence. But at school, George had let his insults against Jefferson fly.

She followed Jefferson onto the rural highway that would lead straight back to town, accelerating to the posted 50 mph speed. As she drove, she replayed their talk and what it meant for her relationship with Ethan. It sounded like George had wanted her to have an active role in the boy's life, but Eve wasn't sure if that included letting Ethan know she was his mother, a role she desperately wanted to inhabit. After grieving the death of her child for so many years, the miracle of Ethan being alive made her heart sing. But someone was actively trying to harm him—and herself—and she couldn't fathom why. That her uncle had something to do with it she had no doubt, but why would he want to kill her when he said he needed her signature on some papers before she turned twenty-five? That part made no sense to her.

Maybe she should have asked Donahue about it when he called, but she'd been so rattled by his request, her only thought had been to get off the phone. Jefferson had shared what he'd found out about her father's family and the fact they apparently thought she was dead. She agreed with Jefferson that calling Trigon Precision to find out who was handling the estate would be a good idea, one she would do first thing Monday morning.

As the road curved to the right, she tapped the brakes to slow from fifty, but the car didn't decelerate.

She depressed the brake pedal harder, her hands tightening on the wheel as the turn sharpened. Panic beat inside her chest, but she refused to give in as she roared closer to Jefferson's car. Pumping the brakes did nothing to slow her SUV, so she wrenched the wheel to the left, directing the car off the road to avoid plowing into Jefferson and Ethan.

The screech of metal against trees echoed as the SUV bounced over the rough terrain. She used all the driving skills she possessed to avoid slamming into trees, but the downward sloop of the verge did little to slow her speed. Up ahead stood a thicker cluster of tall, sturdy oak and hickory trees. *Please God, protect me!*

With a mighty yank on the steering wheel, she managed to

turn the careening vehicle to the left before it slammed into several trees. Her head snapped back, then struck the window as the airbag deployed. Darkness rimmed her vision as the vehicle slid to a stop, but she managed to keep her eyes cracked. She would not pass out.

"Eve?"

The frantic voice of Jefferson reached through the fog and tapped her on the shoulder. Eve pried her eyes open, a groan escaping her as pain radiated along her left arm and head. Where was she?

Jefferson called her name again, his voice muffled slightly, as the previous events filtered slowly back into focus. The hospital. Ethan. The brakes not working.

She started to turn her head to the right toward the passenger side door but stopped herself. Her body ached all over. She didn't think her injuries were life-threatening, but she couldn't be sure. Best to keep her neck and head as still as possible, along with her left arm. She moved her right hand from her lap toward the ignition button. Shutting off the vehicle should unlock the doors. Batting the deflated airbag away, she connected with the ignition button and pushed. The engine stopped and the door locks disengaged with a click.

Jefferson must have heard the sound because the passenger door immediately opened, bringing the scent of gasoline and metal to her nose. "Eve! Are you okay?"

"I don't know. I don't want to move too much. My head hurts and so does my left arm. Where's Ethan?"

"He's fine."

"You didn't leave him in the car alone, did you?" She couldn't bear it if something happened to Ethan because of her accident.

"No, he's with Mrs. Sneedgrass."

"The town librarian?" Maybe she'd hit her head harder than she thought because that didn't make any sense.

"Yes, she was on her way to her daughter's and saw you fly off the road. She stopped and called 911, then offered to wait in the car with Ethan while I went to check on you." He touched her right hand. "What happened?"

"No brakes." She suppressed a shudder at the memory of pressing down on the pedal and meeting no resistance.

"Did you have any problems on your way to the hospital?"

"None." Someone must have tampered with her brakes in the hospital parking garage.

Out of the corner of her eye, Jefferson leaned back. "I hear sirens."

Good, she wanted to get out of this death trap. "Go wait with Ethan. I'll be okay."

"I don't want to leave you."

That he cared about her warmed her heart, but she worried about Ethan. "Please. I'd rather know Ethan is safe."

He hesitated as the sirens grew louder.

"Help is nearly here," she prodded.

"If you're sure."

"I am."

He left the door open as the sirens screamed to a halt. She waited, alternating between praying for herself and for Ethan. Within minutes of Jefferson's departure, two paramedics arrived.

"You're not going to give us trouble, are you, Dr. Davenport?" The tall, skinny man with a tattoo of an eagle covering half of his bald head raised his bushy eyebrows.

Eve would have smiled had she the energy. "Not on your life, Keeson. As long as you behave yourself and not tell any of your dad jokes."

"I can't promise you that."

His partner, a burly black man with his dreadlocks in a ponytail, conferred with Keeson in voice too low for Eve to hear.

"Well, doc, looks like we're gonna have to take you out through the passenger side. I'm going to crawl in the back and see what you've done to yourself, then we'll figure out how to move you."

"I know I'm in good hands with you." Eve closed her eyes as the vehicle shifted with Keeson's weight as he climbed into the backseat. Within a short time, Eve had been assessed and loaded onto a gurney that Keeson and his partner wielded with ease around the numerous trees and undergrowth to the road.

Beside the ambulance, Jefferson stood talking with a sheriff's deputy. A tow truck idled behind the deputy's vehicle. Jefferson broke off his conversation when Keeson wheeled the gurney to the back.

"Eve! How are you?"

In pain, but she wasn't going say so. "Glad to be out of the vehicle."

"I told Deputy Arnold about your brakes, and he'll have the tow truck driver take your vehicle to the forensic lab in Staunton to take a look."

"Good."

Keeson returned from opening the back doors. "We need to get to the hospital to check out the doc here."

"Right." Jefferson hesitated, then stepped back. "I'll take Ethan home and…"

"Stay there with him. I'll call you once they've poked and prodded me." She put as much steel behind her words as she could to convince Jefferson she'd be okay without him hovering at her side. Although she had to admit, she liked having him close.

"If you're sure."

"I am." She waved her right hand toward the ambulance. "I believe my chariot awaits."

Keeson grinned. "Indeed it does, milady." He and his

partner collapsed the wheels as they loaded the gurney into the back.

Eve caught a glimpse of Jefferson watching the process before he turned away as Keeson closed the doors while his partner got into the driver's seat. "Why didn't you let him come with you?"

"Because he has his son with him, and his son was just released from the hospital."

Keeson nodded. "That makes sense, but man, did he want to come with you."

"I guess." She shifted on the bed as the pain in her arm intensified.

"Ain't no guessing about it. That man's in love with you."

Eve refrained from shaking her head at the absurdity of Keeson's claim. She had been grateful she and Jefferson were no longer adversaries, but not hating each other was a long way from love. She must have spoken that thought out loud because Keeson snorted.

"Girl, don't you know hate is the opposite side of the coin from love? I'm telling you, he's head over heels for you."

"If you say so." Eve wasn't about to argue with Keeson, who always enjoyed sharing his varied opinions on many subjects. The paramedic sometimes worked the same shift she did at the mobile clinic, and his rapport with the farm workers made him a favorite.

Keeson regaled her with stories from his last ambulance run while he monitored her condition. All too soon, the ambulance pulled into the hospital emergency department, and she was indeed being poked and prodded. The ER doc, an older man with a weathered face and a no-nonsense manner, proclaimed her arm was bruised but unbroken after viewing the x-ray and her head concussed. He wrapped her arm in an elastic bandage and ordered her to stay overnight for observation. Eve thought about protesting the overnight accommodations, but decided Jefferson had his hands full with Ethan without worrying about her.

Several hours later, alone in her room, she texted Jefferson, glad the deputy had thought to grab her belongings from her SUV and drop them off at the hospital before having the vehicle towed. She told Jefferson she would be staying the night and not to worry. He gave her an update on Ethan, who had eaten a scrambled egg and toast with butter before falling asleep watching *Teen Titans*. He also informed her the Shenandoah County Sheriff's Office would station a deputy outside her door for protection, despite not knowing for sure that someone had tampered with her brakes. Eve was sure Jefferson had insisted on the guard.

While sure she wouldn't sleep a wink with her headache building and her arm aching, Eve settled back to spend a long night thinking about who might want to kill her and Ethan—and why.

AFTER DROPPING ETHAN OFF AT A CLASSMATE'S HOME—AND sharing with the parents why a police officer would be parked outside their home—Jefferson drove to the hospital to pick up Eve, who had texted she would be released that afternoon. It had taken all his willpower not to accompany her to the hospital after the accident, but she had been right to insist he take Ethan home. While she had protested his coming to pick her up, he had simply hung up rather than argue. The need to see her, hold her if he was being honest, overwhelmed him, and he pressed down on the accelerator, willing the miles to fly by.

Sharing with her what George had done had been difficult but freeing too. He hoped she felt the same, and that they could come up with a way to co-parent Ethan, once they could tell him Eve was his mother. His heart whispered maybe they could be a real family, but he couldn't think about romance, not when someone was trying to hurt or take his son. The hospital came into view, and he slowed, startled to see how fast he'd been going in his quest to see Eve.

Once on her floor, he hustled down the corridor, weaving around nurses and other visitors. Turning the corner, his pulse skyrocketed at the sight of a tall man with his back to Jefferson.

"I have every right to see my niece!"

Jefferson's heart stuttered as Ronan Donahue's voice rose, fury dripping from every word. He raced toward the men, Eve's stories about her uncle's cruelties propelling him forward.

"I am not leaving here until I speak to Eve."

"Sir, you need step back." The deputy's firm tone did little to mitigate Donahue's agitation. "If you don't, I will have to arrest you."

"You do not know who you are dealing with," Donahue growled.

"But I do." Jefferson inserted himself into the confrontation with the man who had hurt Eve and deceived them all about Ethan. "Why don't we get a cup of coffee, and you can tell me why you're so eager to see your niece."

Donahue bristled, the shamrock tattoo on the side of his neck drawing Jefferson's attention and reminding him of Eve's assertion her uncle was behind the kidnapping attempts and the brick through her window.

"You're not getting access to Eve until you can explain why you're here." Jefferson held the older man's stare until Donahue nodded. He turned to the deputy. "Please tell Dr. Davenport her uncle came by and where we're going."

The deputy agreed, and Jefferson gestured for Donahue to lead the way to the elevator. The two men didn't speak until they'd gotten coffee and snagged a table in the corner of the busy cafeteria. As Jefferson sipped his beverage, he studied the other man. Fine lines fanned out from his mouth and eyes, and his jaw ticked as if the man was holding his emotions in check. The confidence with which Donahue had always carried himself appeared to have vanished and left a facsimile of that man in its place.

Donahue slapped a brown envelope on the table. "I need Eve to sign a few documents."

"I believe she said to send them to her attorney." Jefferson wanted him to understand Eve had informed him of Donahue's request.

"Yeah, well, it's not something we need to get lawyers involved with. It's family business."

"Family business," Jefferson repeated. "Interesting thing, families. Like the fact Eve's father's family thinks she's dead."

Donahue blanched. "What do you mean?"

"Exactly what I said. Her paternal grandfather, Owen Brandt III, died ten days ago, and his obituary listed his son Nigel Brandt, daughter-in-law Maeve Brandt, and daughter Eve as predeceasing him. I wondered why."

"I have no idea." Donahue picked up his cup and took a sip.

Jefferson switched topics. "Let me see the papers."

"No, they're for Eve." Donahue placed a hand on top of the envelope while taking another gulp of his beverage.

"Why did you tell her Ethan had died?"

Donahue choked on the liquid. Jefferson didn't say anything else while the other man regained his composure.

"If that's how she wants to remember it..." His voice trailed off, giving Jefferson a glimpse of the man who had sat in his parents' living room and sorrowfully told them about Eve's decision. "She didn't want the baby."

"No, you wanted to get rid of the baby." Jefferson was done with playing nice. This man might be behind the attacks, and he wanted to know why. "You needed Eve to be alone, isolated, but when she turned eighteen and left, you let her go. Until now. What's so important about her turning twenty-five?"

Donahue's mouth firmed, but he didn't elucidate the reason for his visit.

Jefferson sipped more coffee as he sifted through possible scenarios in his mind. Then he recalled Eve's assertion Donahue had spent the $5 million insurance payout from her parents' death, and a possibility popped into his brain. "That $5 million must not have lasted too long."

"What?" Donahue frowned.

"The insurance money from the death of Eve's parents."

A slight flush reddened his cheeks, leading Jefferson to believe he was on the right track.

"She didn't tell you? She found out about the money when applying to medical school. Where did it all go? Certainly not to Eve."

"Lorraine and I cared for her since she was a toddler. Clothes and food don't come cheap."

"How much food and clothing could one girl require?" Jefferson leaned forward. "Especially when you didn't even feed her lunch."

His barb hit home as the other man's eyes widened, but Donahue ignored the bait. "We were her legal guardians, entitled to spend the money as we saw fit."

The mention of money brought another idea into Jefferson's mind, and he snatched the envelope from under Donahue's hand.

"Hey, that's mine!"

His shout brought the attention of several nearby tables, and Jefferson used the attention to slide the single sheet of paper from the envelope. "Disclaimer of Inheritance" read the top sheet, but Donahue lunged across the table and grabbed the paper before Jefferson could skim it. Then the other man left the cafeteria, heading toward the outside exit. Jefferson tossed the remains of his coffee into the trashcan and went back upstairs to Eve. Finding out more about Owen Brandt's will became top priority, because if he wasn't mistaken, the inheritance Donahue wanted Eve to disclaim involved the Brandt estate.

Outside her door, he thanked the deputy for keeping Donahue out before knocking on the door. At Eve's invitation, he entered to find her dressed in scrubs, a clear plastic bag with yesterday's clothes by her side.

"The deputy said my uncle stopped by?" Eve gathered her things. "How did he know I was in the hospital?"

"He didn't say, and I forgot to ask." He mentally slapped himself for not finding out. With the deputy following them, the trip to Twin Oaks went off without a hitch. During the drive to Twin Oaks, Jefferson filled Eve in about the inheritance disclaimer Donahue wanted her to sign.

"You think it has to do with my grandfather's death." Eve grasped what Jefferson had concluded.

"Yes. I think we should try to reach someone at the company." He braked at an all-way stop while a farmer with a load of hay in a trailer turned left. "It must be connected to the will somehow, but why would Donahue want you to sign a paper that would disinherit you? I did bring up the $5 million insurance policy, and he didn't deny keeping the money."

"That doesn't make sense. You'd think he would want me to sign something giving him control over any money I would inherit from my grandfather."

"Unless…" Jeff didn't complete the thought as he accelerated, his mind working on fitting together all the pieces from what they'd learned so far.

"Unless someone is paying him more to keep me from coming forward with a claim on the estate."

He tapped the steering wheel as he mulled over Eve's statement. "That might be true, but that would mean someone close to your grandfather has known about you for years."

Eve nodded, her eyes brightening as her quick mind latched onto something—a look he remembered well from their school days. "That would explain why I wasn't allowed to have any social media accounts and why my uncle had spyware on my computer. I thought he was being mean like usual, but what if it was to prevent my father's family from finding out I wasn't dead? All his actions kept me tethered to him, and he only allowed me to be with you because you didn't have social media accounts."

"I didn't particularly find those sites interesting, but George did. He followed some influencers but didn't bother posting much." She might be onto something as he turned her theory over in his mind, searching for flaws.

"I bet someone was paying him to keep me hidden away all these years."

"Maybe, but that still doesn't answer the biggest question —why now? What triggered the person to move from wanting you out of sight to killing you and kidnapping or hurting Ethan?" Those questions bounced around in his head like a metal ball in an old-fashioned arcade game.

"Because my grandfather died. It must have something to do with his will or estate or something."

"I suppose that makes sense, but if your grandfather thought you were dead, then surely there could be nothing for you to inherit." He slowed as they entered Twin Oaks.

"It could be the will was written in a way that didn't name specific heirs, only said things like 'my children' or 'my grandchildren' or 'any of my offspring and their descendants.' Those types of things would mean if I returned from the dead, I could inherit like the rest of them."

Jefferson pulled into his driveway. "Let's see what we can uncover and test your theory."

He waved to the deputy, who had accompanied them

home and now turned his vehicle around to head back to the county. A Twin Oaks police cruiser glided up to park at the curb, and Jefferson was glad they still had protection, although he knew that wouldn't last much longer, given the small force. Twin Oaks didn't have much crime, but that didn't mean the department could spare officers for protection duty indefinitely.

Inside, he texted the parents of Ethan's classmate to say they were home, and the mom responded with news the boys were building with LEGOs and could Ethan stay for pizza, after which they'd bring him home. He gave his permission, noting he and Eve would have several hours to research her family without any distractions. As he heated water for tea and Eve checked on Willoughby, he reflected how natural it seemed for her to be in this house. For a few hours, he could pretend they belonged together.

FOURTEEN

E ve stretched her arms over her head, then did some side stretches to relieve the kinks in her muscles. They had been able to piece together a family tree from newspaper articles and the Trigon Precision website, but since her grandfather's will hadn't cleared probate yet, they still had no clue who benefited.

"More questions than answers." She carried her empty tea mug to the sink. "I hate suspecting uncles, aunts, and cousins I've never met of wanting me and Ethan permanently removed. Especially because I always wanted siblings and a large extended family."

That's what hurt the most—the fact her uncle had denied her the chance to know her father's family. Her uncle had only had her mother, as their parents had died and been only children themselves. Why hadn't her father's family contacted Donahue? Maybe they had and he'd brushed them off. Perhaps he had even been the one to tell them of her demise along with her parents.

"About the only thing I can offer for dinner is pizza." Jefferson ran a hand through his hair. "I need to get to the store."

That was something she could solve. "Do you have a list?"

"I started one, so let me see if I can find it." He hunted for it, moving papers and opening a few drawers before he found the scrap of paper. "Seems to have enough to get us through the next few days."

She held out her hand, and he gave it to her. A quick glance showed it had the usual suspects—milk, bread, eggs, etc. She snapped a pic of it with her phone, then opened a text to the owner of the Twin Oaks General Store. "Do you like lamb curry?"

"Yes."

She added two orders of the curry, plus a request for delivery, then hit send. "Terrance at the general store delivers. Plus, it's Monday, which means his wife is making her curries. I'm partial to the lamb, but her chicken and goat curries are amazing as well."

"Goat curry?"

She laughed at his dubious tone. "Don't knock it 'til you try it, buster. It's quite tasty." Her phone buzzed, and she checked the incoming text. "Dinner—and your groceries— will be here in thirty minutes."

His stomach rumbled. "Good thing, because I'm suddenly starving."

"Should we wait to eat until you get Ethan?"

"Nah, he's having pizza with the Clarks, and they'll bring him home around seven."

Which meant she and Jefferson had nearly two more hours to themselves. A shiver slithered down her spine as she relished the thought of being alone with him. Maybe after the meal, they'd carry cups of decaf coffee to the couch. Jefferson would slip his arm around her, and she'd snuggle against him like she had a million times before when she'd thought she would have forever with him.

"Eve?"

She blinked, coming back to earth with a bump. "Sorry, did you ask me something?"

"I found the law firm that handles Trigon Precision's matters." He turned his laptop toward her to show the website for Thomas & Associates Law Firm based in Phoenix. "I think we should call."

She calculated the time difference. It was only late afternoon in Arizona. "Sure, but maybe you should pretend to be my attorney or something? I'm a little nervous about calling myself."

"Good idea. I'm sure I can sound lawyerly." Jefferson winked, then dialed the number on his cell. He put it on speaker as it rang.

"Thomas & Associates, how may I help you?" said a pleasant feminine voice.

"Good afternoon. I'm Mr. Smith, representing the interests of Owen Brandt's granddaughter." Jefferson paused, his eyebrows raised as if telling Eve he would wait for the other woman to say something.

"That is not being handled by our office. You'll need to call Vickers & Sawyers over in Flagstaff."

"Thank you." He disconnected. "I forgot to ask if your uncle formally adopted you, since your last name wasn't Brandt but Donahue."

"I thought he had since my birth certificate lists my last name as Donahue and not Brandt, but now I wonder if that's true."

"We'll stick to saying your last name's Brandt for now to avoid confusion. Would you find the law office number for me?"

Eve Googled Vickers & Sawyers, then rattled off the number for Jefferson. Again she waited, trying to curb her impatience as the line rang eight times before the receptionist picked up, then transferred Jefferson to someone else.

"Vickers & Sawyers." The clipped male voice wasn't as welcoming as the Thomas & Associates receptionist had been.

Jefferson repeated his opening line.

"Which granddaughter?"

"To whom am I speaking, please?"

"Dave Clemens, an associate in the firm. I'm working with Mr. Vickers on the Brandt estate."

Jefferson shot Eve a look, and she nodded, giving him permission to use her name.

"Eve Brandt, Nigel Brandt's daughter."

The man sucked in a breath. "Who is this?"

"My name is Jefferson Smith."

Clemens didn't let him get anything else out. "I'm not sure what you think you're trying to pull, but Eve Brandt is dead, has been for more than twenty years."

Now it was Eve's turn to gasp at the confirmation of what they'd read in the obit. "I'm not dead."

"Please stop calling." Clemens hung up.

"That didn't go well." Jefferson tapped his phone against his leg.

"What do we do now?" Frustration reared its head and chomped down on her fraying nerves.

"We have learned two important things." He held up a finger. "First, you are indeed Owen Brandt's granddaughter."

"But we already knew that from the obit."

"And two, that someone else has contacted the firm about you."

She reran the short conversation with the associate, reframing his words in light of what Jefferson said. "He said to stop calling, as if we'd called before."

"Exactly."

The doorbell rang in concert with her phone vibrating. She checked the text. "Food's here."

"I'll get it." Jefferson took a step toward the door, then paused. "You might want to call your attorney friend."

"I'll get in touch with David right now." Within minutes, she'd connected with David Keener, a local attorney who handled everything from estate planning and wills to the occasional civil lawsuit. By the time Jefferson had put away the groceries and plated the curry, David had promised to be at their house around eight to discuss their options. For the first time since running into Ethan and Jefferson, a sense that they might be making progress in figuring out what was happening filled her with peace. Then maybe, just maybe, they were seeing the light at the end of the tunnel and would find answers to their questions.

"THANKS FOR COMING BY, DAVID." EVE SHUT THE DOOR BEHIND the lawyer as he left, then turned to Jefferson. "What do you think?"

He thought the attorney had been entirely too friendly with Eve, despite the other man's wedding ring. The pair had shared several chuckles about past situations Jefferson hadn't been around for, making him wish David would hurry up and leave. Ethan had requested Eve join Jefferson in his bedtime ritual, reinforcing the family feeling that had been growing in Jefferson's heart since Eve had moved in a couple of days ago. With her cabin uninhabitable after the fire, he had held his breath she wouldn't want to leave right away.

"Jefferson?"

His name brought his thoughts back to the conversation at hand, but when his gaze met hers, he completely forgot what they had been discussing. Instead, memories of the past collided with the present, fueling his growing fantasy about a future with Eve by his side helping to raise Ethan. His blood hummed her name, pushing him to step closer. "You're so beautiful."

"I am?" The wonder and doubt in her voice made him bold.

"Yes, you are to me." He gently grazed his fingers across her cheek, tucking a strand of hair into place behind one ear. "You were a knockout in high school and your beauty has only grown."

"Even with my bruised arm and face abrasion from the airbag deployment?"

"Those are temporary."

"My big nose isn't." She wrinkled the appendage as if in jest, but her eyes were serious.

He ran a finger down her supposedly large nose. "It seems perfect to me."

Her breath hitched as he trailed his finger along her jawline. "And my smile?"

"Takes my breath away." His own heartrate accelerated as he concentrated on her mouth. Would it be as soft as he remembered?

Her body swayed closer to his. "Jefferson?"

His name on those sweet lips again. "Hmm?"

"I'd like to find out too." She held his gaze, her irises darkening.

He took her response to mean she would be open to his kiss but played out their verbal exchange a bit longer. "You would?" He threaded his fingers through her hair at the back of her neck, drawing her face nearer to his own. "So would I."

"Then what are you waiting for?" Her breath fanned his face, filling his senses with her very essence, a scent he'd known well at one time.

He closed the distance with a soft growl, stopping a hair's breadth away from her slightly parted lips. "You're sure?" He hoped she realized what he was asking, that he wanted more than a kiss from her. That he hoped this would be the new beginning for both of them, and for Ethan.

In answer, she bridged the scant inch between them and

placed her mouth on his. The kiss was everything he'd remembered and so much more. The contours of her lips held familiarity yet unplowed territory.

A faint sound penetrated his senses, drawing him back from the dream of holding Eve in his arms once more. She pulled back, cocking her head as his ragged breath filled the space. Then he registered the noise—Ethan screaming.

Jefferson dropped his arms and ran for the stairs, Eve right behind him. "Ethan!" How could he have let his guard down? If anything happened to his son.... He burst into Ethan's room, bracing to fight off yet another intruder, but the room held only his sobbing son. "Ethan, what is it?"

The boy threw himself into Jefferson's arms. "The bad dream again."

"Oh, sweetheart, it's okay. I'm here now." He rubbed Ethan's back as Eve slipped into the room.

"Dr. Eve?" Ethan twisted out of Jefferson's arms, tears flowing freely down his wet cheeks. "I was so scared."

"Your dad's here now." She tousled his hair, and he grabbed her hand.

"I want you." The plaintive note in his voice coupled with the hiccupping sobs were no match for Jefferson. Ethan wanted Eve, instinctively sought her out, and he wouldn't stand in the way.

"Sure, buddy." He stood and gestured for Eve to take his spot. She hesitated, her expression hidden in the room's shadows. But when Ethan tugged her hand, she sank down onto the bed beside him.

Ethan leaned into her, and she shifted to sit with her back against the headboard. For a few minutes, she hummed softly while his sobs lessened. She smoothed the hair back on his forehead. "What makes your dream so scary?"

"The man. He tries to grab me." Ethan shuddered. "It seems so real."

"You mean the man who came through the window?"

"No, not the recent ones. This is an old dream that comes back sometimes."

Eve darted a glance at Jefferson, who knew she'd have questions for him later, but she merely asked Ethan to describe the dream.

"I never see his face, but he tries to grab me from my bed and take me somewhere away from my dad."

"Always from your bed?"

"In our old house, the one I lived in with Granny and Papaw."

"When you lived with your first dad?"

"Yes, before my first dad died."

Jefferson recalled George saying Ethan had started having nightmares before the car accident, but Ethan hadn't ever connected this particular one with Boston. He held his tongue and let Eve continue her gentle questioning. She took her son through the dream, the outlines of which were very familiar to Jefferson.

Ethan wrapped his arms around Eve's neck. "I wish you were my mommy."

Jefferson strained to hear Eve's reply. They had agreed earlier in talking with David to keep Eve's motherhood of Ethan a secret for now, although from the attempts on Ethan's life, it appeared someone knew or suspected as much.

"You know who's even better than a mommy?"

Her question made Ethan loosen his hold and lean back. "Who?"

"Jesus." She paused for a few seconds, then added, "Let's pray."

"Okay." Ethan sniffled, then peered around her. "Dad?"

"I'm here." Jefferson sank onto the bed on the other side of Ethan, who promptly took his hand.

"You have to hold Dr. Eve's hand too, so we'll be a circle."

Jefferson took Eve's in his own, giving it a squeeze as she led them in prayer for Ethan's safety and that his son would have no more nightmares. As she prayed, Jefferson thanked God for reuniting Ethan with his mother—and him with the love of his life. He added his own prayer that God would grant him the desires of his heart and let them find their happily ever after together.

CHAPTER

FIFTEEN

Eve hummed as she washed her hands after examining a six-year-old with a sore throat. This time, it was strep, so she'd prescribed an antibiotic.

"You're in a good mood for a busy Tuesday." Lily paused with a sheaf of papers in her hands.

"Am I?" Eve couldn't stop the grin from spreading across her face as her body warmed in remembrance of Jefferson's amazing, spectacular kiss. That and Ethan wanting her to be his mommy. It had taken all of Eve's willpower not to blurt out she was his mother, but she agreed with Jefferson that it would be best to keep her identity from Ethan until they had discovered who was behind the attacks and attempted kidnappings.

Lily narrowed her eyes. "You kissed him."

"What? Who?" Eve had forgotten how perceptive her friend could be.

"Don't play Miss Innocent with me. You. Kissed. Jefferson."

Before Eve could respond, one of the nurses came up. "Dr. Davenport, Kyle's mother called to say his fever hasn't gone down despite the use of fever reducers."

"Can we squeeze him in this morning?"

The nurse consulted her tablet. "Maybe after the physical scheduled for twelve-forty-five?"

"Have Kyle come in at one." Another sandwich at her desk wouldn't hurt her, but seeing the sick nine-year-old took priority over leaving the office for lunch.

After the nurse left to make the call to Kyle's mother, Lily planted one hand on her hip. "Don't think we're done with this conversation."

"I don't kiss and tell." Eve winked, then hurried off to the next patient, ignoring Lily's hoot of laughter. The morning flew by, and it wasn't until nearly one-thirty that Eve dropped into her desk chair with her office door closed to grab a few minutes of solitude and gobble down the Cuban sandwich Lily had brought her from the Pink Pig. Despite it becoming cold, she savored the roasted pork, ham, and melted cheese with the tang of the spicy mustard and crunch of the still-crispy pickles. She'd only eaten half the sandwich when her office door burst open and her uncle charged in the room.

"I will see my niece!" Ronan Donahue roared as Lily attempted to snag his sleeve.

"Sir, you can't barge in here like this. I'm calling the police," Lily held up her phone.

"Lily, it's okay." Eve rewrapped her sandwich as if she had all the time in the world as the man across from her trembled with some emotion. Anger, definitely, given his flushed face and clenched jaw. But something else lurked behind the rage, as her uncle very rarely lost control even when he was mad. This was a man on the brink, who needed something desperately. "Please, have a seat."

Her cordial tone must have confused him because he glanced down at the envelope in his hand, then at her, his eyes a swirling mix of receding anger and fear. That was it. Ronan Donahue, the man who had never shown fear in all her life, was afraid.

"I'll be with you in a moment. I need to check on my schedule, as you caught me at the tail end of my lunch break." Eve didn't give him time to react, but slipped out the door, leaving it cracked to keep an eye on her uncle. To Lily, she whispered, "Call Jefferson to let him know my uncle's here, then see if David Keener can come by."

"David's here."

"Why?" She couldn't believe her attorney would be here right when she needed him.

"He brought in Holly to get a rash looked at. Noelle took her grandmother to see her grandfather today."

"Good." Eve sucked in a breath. "I mean, not good Holly has a rash, but good that David's here. Would you…"

"Hold that darling baby while you tackle Mr. Meanie in there with David's help? Certainly." Lily punched in a number. "Calling Jefferson now, and I'll send David back immediately."

"You're the best." Eve pushed the door open and re-entered her office. Her uncle slumped in the chair facing her desk. She left the door ajar, then dropped into her chair. "I heard you tried to see me in the hospital."

"Yeah, but Jefferson Smith wouldn't allow me to talk with you." His hand trembled as he held out the envelope. "I need you to sign these papers."

"I'll be happy to read them over once my attorney gets here." Eve studied the man who had terrorized her as a young child. She had thought about this meeting in the years since she'd wiggled out from under his harsh thumb but had never imagined it would be in these circumstances. Gone was the man who had ruled her life with an iron fist. In his place was a man on the edge, desperation and fear clinging to him like barnacles.

Her door opened and David came inside. "Dr. Davenport, Ms. Turnbolt said you wanted to see me?"

"Yes, let me introduce you to my uncle, Ronan Donahue from Boston. Uncle, this is my lawyer, David Keener."

Donahue mumbled something but didn't shake David's outstretched hand. "Why'd you have to bring a lawyer into it? I just need your signature on these papers." His voice rose as anger once more brought color to his cheeks.

David held out his hand toward her uncle for the papers. The two men had a staring contest that lasted nearly a full minute, as Eve ticked off the seconds on her large wall clock. Then Donahue capitulated and gave the envelope to the younger man. David pulled out the papers and read them silently while no one spoke.

"Dr. Davenport, I must advise you not to sign these papers."

"You have no right!" Her uncle leapt to his feet, his hands making fists as if he would strike the other man. "This is between me and my niece."

"But she's not your niece."

David's remark floored Eve. "What do you mean I'm not his niece?"

David kept staring straight at the man Eve had called uncle her entire life. "I had a very interesting conversation with an associate at the law firm handling your grandfather's estate. It turns out your mother wasn't Ronan Donahue's sister after all. His sister had the same first name as your mother—Maeve—but Maeve Donahue died of breast cancer in her mid-twenties before you were born."

Eve sagged against her chair, her mind spinning so fast, she could hardly catch hold of a thought. "Then how, why?" She couldn't even form a question, not even sure what she was asking.

"That's the million-dollar question, isn't it? Or, should I say, the five-million-dollar question." David briefly met Eve's gaze, compassion and surety in his own. "I'm still in the early stages of my investigation, but I suspect Mr. Donahue and

Nigel Brandt met and formed some sort of partnership. Your father lived a pretty wild youth and young adult life, becoming the black sheep of the Brandt family. His father—Owen Brandt—kicked him out of the family business when Nigel embezzled funds and fled Arizona. How am I doing so far, Mr. Donahue?"

Her uncle—no, her father's business associate?—hung his head. Eve thought he wouldn't answer, but then he said, "I met Nigel in Vegas, where he was throwing money around like confetti at the craps table but not winning much. When his funds ran low, we decided to make our luck elsewhere and became partners."

"In some rather interesting schemes that weren't quite legal, am I right?" David interjected.

Donahue shrugged. "Doesn't matter, as I'm ruined anyway. We had a pretty good run for a while, then Nigel met and married Maeve Turner and decided to go straight. He moved to Indiana, where you came along. But then his past must have caught up with him, and he called me to say they were leaving town and would I look after Maeve and you if anything happened to him."

"Convenient that he had taken out such a large insurance policy a month before he and Maeve died in a car accident," David said.

"Wasn't convenient to me." Donahue threw Eve a look of annoyance. "You weren't the one saddled with a toddler."

"I'll bet the insurance payout eased some of the discomfort."

Donahue ignored David's comment. "By then I had settled in Boston, and Lorraine wasn't happy with raising a kid. With my sister's name the same as your mother's, it made sense to pass you off as our niece. I knew someone who could doctor your birth certificate to give you our last name. That way, no one asked many questions."

Eve fought to keep her emotions in check. The confirmation of her childhood fears that she was an imposition, that her uncle and aunt didn't really love her, threatened to overwhelm her. "And the cruelties you and Lorraine inflicted on me? What was that for? Some kind of payback for my father's terrible judgment in making you my guardian?"

"It wasn't personal." Donahue seemed to have recovered a bit of his old bravado. "I had to make sure you wouldn't blab or ask too many questions."

That didn't make any sense. "But you were my legal guardian according to my parents' will. I didn't know the difference, so what could I possibly tell and who would I have told?"

But Donahue firmed his lips and didn't answer her questions. "You're not going to sign the papers."

"That would renounce any claim from her on Owen Brandt's estate?" David clarified.

Anger at his trying to steal her inheritance crept up, but she batted it down. Then she thought of his lies about Ethan and the danger her son was in. She had no doubt this man was capable of hiring someone to kidnap Ethan. "Is that why you're trying to kidnap and hurt my son?"

Jefferson paused outside Eve's office door to gauge the temperature of the conversation before entering. Lily had informed him upon his arrival that David was with Eve, so she wasn't facing her uncle alone. No raised voices, a good sign and one he hoped would continue. He checked to see if Detective Cunningham had responded to his text letting her know of Ronan Donahue's arrival but had no new messages.

He'd sent Ethan to school with the assurance that a Twin Oaks police officer would be stationed in a patrol car at the school and the resource officer would keep a close eye on the Ethan's second grade class throughout the day. He couldn't keep his son home indefinitely, but he also couldn't shake the sense that the danger to Ethan was far from over.

"Why would I do that?" Donahue's voice, while raised, held not anger but confusion.

Jefferson pushed open the door as Eve said, "Because you want to keep the inheritance for yourself."

"I can't inherit anything." Donahue wiped sweat from his brow.

"Then why are you trying to force her to sign that paper?" David's question seemed to make the older man even more uncomfortable.

Jefferson slipped around the lawyer to be next to Eve, who stood behind her desk facing her uncle. She reached for his hand, and he gladly accepted hers, warming her ice-cold fingers between his palms.

"Because…" Donahue licked his lips. "I, uh…"

Eve frowned, her forehead crinkling as she stared at the man who had made her life so miserable. "Are you okay?"

"I'm fine." But the sheen of sweat on his forehead gave lie to the statement.

Eve broke away from Jefferson's hold to round the desk, going to the man sitting in the chair. "Does your chest feel tight?"

"What?" Donahue blinked as if trying to focus on his niece. "I don't know…"

Eve met Jefferson's gaze, hers troubled. "Call 911 and tell them we have a male in his fifties experiencing the symptoms of a heart attack."

Jefferson peered at Donahue, noting the ashen complexion, and dialed. Could someone fake a heart attack? Maybe, but Donahue didn't strike him as someone with that much acting ability.

"Let's get you on the floor, shall we?" Eve's tone commanded obedience, and her uncle acquiesced to her instructions like a docile lamb, entirely out of character to his earlier bluster. Maybe he really was having some sort of episode.

He turned his back to concentrate on the 911 dispatcher. After answering her general questions, he told her the patient was with a doctor to forestall any attempt on the dispatcher's part to walk him through CPR. David stepped back into the room with an AED Eve must have sent him to get while Jefferson was talking to the dispatcher.

Eve had Donahue on his back, his feet slightly elevated and his eyes closed. A light blanket covered him, and she listened to his heart through her stethoscope.

"ETA for the ambulance is about five minutes."

"Thanks." She sat up, her expression less-than-pleased.

"Is he going to be okay?" Jefferson pitched his voice low in order to not disturb Donahue, whose complexion had waxed even paler.

"I don't know. His heart rate isn't as steady as I'd like, but I've done what I can do for now." She sighed. "He wanted me to sign a paper giving up my rights to Owen Brandt's money. It doesn't make any sense. What would my uncle, who's not really my uncle—get out of it?"

"Money." David's succinct comment drew their attention away from the man on the floor.

Lily, holding David's fussing baby, came into the room. "She wants her daddy."

David took the infant from the office manager. "There, there. Daddy's here."

"The ambulance will be here soon. Please direct them to my office and assure the other patients it's not a child who needs the care," Eve told her.

Lily nodded, then said to David, "The nurse practitioner can see you, if you come this way." Lily guided them out of the office, pulling the door closed with a soft click.

Eve inserted the earpieces on her stethoscope and listened to Donahue's heart again as Jefferson mulled over what the lawyer had said. Money. Not from Eve's inheritance but from someone else, someone who would benefit with one less person to split a very large pie. When she removed the stethoscope, he tried out his hypothesis. "What if Donahue is being paid to disinherit you?"

"But he can't inherit in my stead because he's not a blood relative." She flexed her wrapped left arm, the movement pinching her mouth.

"He's not but whoever's paying him might be."

The sound of wheels along the corridor signaled the arrival of the EMTs. She scrambled to her feet as the door opened and a paramedic entered. "Dr. Eve, what have we got?"

Eve quickly explained Donahue's symptoms and stepped back to allow the EMTs to assess, then load the man onto the gurney. "Which hospital?"

"Staunton General is the best one for heart issues," the lanky EMT told her.

She thanked them, then reached for her cell phone. "I'd better let Lorraine know."

He waited while she made the call, leaving a voicemail for the woman who had shown little love for her during her childhood. Then he returned to the previous topic. "I think we have to consider it's someone who stands to inherit from your grandfather and wouldn't want to share with a long-lost granddaughter."

"Who might that be?" Detective Cunningham said from the doorway. "Your office manager told me to come back."

Eve spread her hands. "That's just it. I have no idea other than the list from the obituary." She ruffled through some papers on her desk and extracted a printout of the obit. "Here you go."

The detective scanned the article for a few minutes. "Your father was one of three siblings with Brandt's first wife."

"That's correct," Eve said.

"With his second wife, he had four more kids." Cunningham tapped the paper. "We need a full list of heirs."

"I think David was getting that info from the Arizona attorneys handling the estate," Eve said. "I can ask him, if he's still here with Holly."

Eve exited her office, leaving Jefferson to explain about the lawyer's sick baby. The detective's phone rang, and she excused herself to answer it.

Eve came back into her office. "He'd already left, and when I called his office, his secretary said he was going to work from home the rest of the day."

Cunningham pocketed her phone, her expression drawn. "Mr. Smith—"

Jefferson didn't let her finish, the sure knowledge that whatever she was about to say involved his son. "What's happened to Ethan?"

"He's been kidnapped."

CHAPTER

SIXTEEN

Jefferson paced the short length of the principal's office, each step a prayer for Ethan's safe return. His son had been missing for two hours, and this time, he held little hope of a quick return. This time, kidnappers with guns had abducted his son as the class returned from outdoor gym. The school's resource officer had done her best to prevent the two masked men from snatching Ethan but had little choice but to focus on keeping the majority of the children safe from the armed intruders.

"Any updates?" Eve's haunted eyes mirrored his own. She wrapped her arms around her middle and shivered despite the elevated temperature in the office that held a variety of police officers and deputies, plus school officials.

"No." Jefferson reached toward her, intending to draw her into his arms. He needed to hold her as much as he suspected she needed his comfort. But before his fingers connected with her arm, Cunningham approached them.

"Dr. Davenport, did your lawyer come up with the list of relatives we discussed at your office?"

Eve swiped tears from her damp cheeks, then fished her phone from her back pocket. "I checked a few minutes ago and there wasn't anything, but let me text him. David was calling the Arizona attorneys to get a full list of beneficiaries to my grandfather's will."

"Thanks." The detective glanced at Jefferson. "How are you holding up?"

"Not too good." He saw no reason to sugar coat his emotions, which vacillated between guilt and fear. He shouldn't have let Ethan go back to school, even with the added protection of two police officers.

"It's not your fault."

Cunningham's words did little to assuage the turmoil roiling inside him. "I didn't want him to go to school until these people were caught, but he missed his friends." He didn't add *and you said he would be safe*. Casting blame would only distract the police from finding Ethan. "Will you call in the FBI?"

The detective shook her head. "We don't suspect Ethan's been taken across the state line, and with the sheriff's office lending its support, we have plenty of manpower to conduct a search. But rest assured, we will call them if we feel it will help find Ethan quicker. For now, we're the ones who know this area and the case the best."

That made sense, but Jefferson wouldn't hesitate to push for the FBI to come if things weren't progressing. So far, they had identified the path the men had taken on foot to where a four-by-four had been waiting in the wooded area behind the school. From there, trackers with canines, law enforcement personnel, and a host of volunteers were following the main paved trail as well as the numerous dirt off shoots. He itched to be out there searching, but Cunningham had convinced him staying at the command center in the school would be more helpful as questions arose.

"Got it." Eve held up her phone. "Is there a printer I can use to print out the list of names?"

Soon Eve distributed copies of the list of beneficiaries to

Cunningham and Jefferson. The list of names blurred as tears clouded his vision. He blinked them away, shoving his worry for Ethan down. Someone on this list likely had his son or was behind the men who had kidnapped him.

"Any name stand out?" Cunningham asked.

Eve shook her head. "I don't know any of these people."

They needed help in narrowing down the who, and Jefferson could think of only one person who could assist. "Donahue."

Eve had called the hospital when she'd arrived at the school with Jefferson and Cunningham, only to be told her uncle was being examined. "I'll call the hospital for an update." She punched in the number, putting the phone on speaker so Jefferson and Cunningham could hear. Once connected, Cunningham identified herself as a member of law enforcement and requested info on Donahue's condition, only to be told he had been rushed into surgery to repair a blocked artery.

Jefferson crumpled the printout of names into a ball, frustration pushing him to do something, anything, to find his son. "What about your aunt?" He and Eve had decided it would make more sense to simply continue referring to the Donahues as her uncle and aunt to avoid unnecessary explanations.

"Lorraine? She hasn't responded to my voicemail, but I'll call her again." Eve did so, again using the speaker function on her phone. This time, her call was answered.

"Hello?" The female voice sounded annoyed.

"Lorraine, it's Eve."

"Are you the one who's been calling me?"

"Yes, to tell you Ronan is in the hospital."

Jefferson admired Eve's calm demeanor in the face of her aunt's obvious irritation.

"Hospital? What are you talking about? Is this another of your tricks? Ronan told me about your recent shenanigans."

Eve raised her eyebrows at the accusation, but her voice stayed steady. "I don't know what Ronan said about me, but he was rushed to Staunton General Hospital because he was having a heart attack. He's in surgery now for a blocked artery."

"What?" Lorraine's tone sharpened. "You did that to him. He told me how you schemed to keep him from getting the money due to him. He's been worried for months since you disappeared and stole all that money from him."

Eve rubbed her forehead. "Lorraine, I have no idea what you're talking about, but I can assure you, I did not take any money."

"Of course you'd say that. You always were a liar." Lorraine huffed. "I bet you're even lying about Ronan and his supposed heart attack."

Cunningham stepped into the conversation. "Mrs. Donahue, this is Detective Cunningham with the Twin Oaks police here in Virginia. Your niece is telling you the truth. Ronan Donahue was taken by ambulance to the hospital for a suspected heart attack. We just confirmed with the hospital minutes ago that he is in surgery."

Silence, then Lorraine let out a string of curses that had every head in the room turning their way. Jefferson put his arm around Eve's shoulders in a vain attempt to shield her from the volley of hate slung by the woman who had raised her. When Lorraine stopped, the detective continued. "Mrs. Donahue, I can appreciate your concern for your husband, but right now, he's in good hands, and we have a little boy missing."

"What has a missing brat have to do with us?"

"We believe your husband was in contact with someone from Arizona about an inheritance."

"Oh, that. Yes, he said something about needing Eve to sign a piece of paper, which, of course, she won't. Always causing trouble, that one."

Jefferson squeezed Eve's shoulders. It must hurt to have your character denigrated by someone who should have been in Eve's corner.

"Do you know the name of the person who contacted Mr. Donahue?"

"I have no idea."

"Mrs. Donahue, a child's life is at stake." Cunningham's tone urged the other woman to cooperate. "If you could check your husband's papers or computer for an email, that would be very helpful."

Over Lorraine's protests, the detective added, "Or we could have someone from the Boston police come by with a search warrant to find the info."

Lorraine ground out an unpleasant word, then said, "I'll check."

Cunningham hit the mute button and turned to Eve. "Wow, your aunt is something else."

"Yep, she certainly is." Eve nestled closer into Jefferson's embrace. "I hope she can find a name so we can rescue Ethan."

"Me too." Jefferson rubbed her arm as he held her, sending another prayer for a break-through.

Five agonizing minutes passed before Lorraine returned to the phone. "I don't have a name, but Ronan was corresponding with someone with an email of hunter0605@gmail.com about the paper for Eve to sign."

"Thank you, Mrs. Donahue." But the other woman had already disconnected the call. Cunningham returned the phone to Eve. "It's not much, but it's better than nothing. I'll get my tech gal to see what she can find."

Eve had jotted down the email address as Lorraine said it. She handed the piece of paper to Cunningham. "Could the numbers be a birth month and date?"

"June fifth? Maybe. We'll see if any of the heirs have that

as their birthday." Cunningham moved toward the door, her phone to her ear.

"What if they don't find him in time?" Eve's question addressed the very one tumbling in Jefferson's mind.

"We will."

Her phone buzzed and she glanced it, the color leaching from her face.

"Eve?"

Her hand shook as she held up the phone for him to read the text.

We have Ethan. If you want him back, come alone to this address. No police. No boyfriend.

EVE SUCKED IN A BREATH AS JEFFERSON READ THE TEXT. "I HAVE to go."

His troubled gaze met hers. "Of course you do, but you can't go alone. It's too dangerous. I"—he swallowed hard—"I couldn't bear to lose you again."

His words thawed some of the ice building inside her after reading the message. She reached for his hand. "I know." She blinked back tears. "I feel the same." She wanted to throw herself into his arms, but another incoming text made her gasp.

You have twenty minutes. Don't be late.

Entering the unfamiliar address into Google Maps put the distance at six miles away with an estimated drive time of eighteen minutes. "There's no time. I have to go now."

Jefferson craned his neck. "Cunningham's not back yet." He took her elbow. "Let me walk you to your rental."

No one paid them any attention as they slipped out the school. "I'm parked by the exit."

"Text Cunningham the location. I'm coming with you."

"No, they said to come alone." Eve wanted him by her

side so much, but she couldn't jeopardize Ethan's safety by having Jefferson tag along.

"Listen to me. It's too dangerous to go by yourself. I will lie down in the backseat and I won't get out until you've gone. I'll count to thirty before exiting the vehicle."

She shook her head, but he interjected, "I will simply follow you if you don't let me do this. He's my son too."

"I know." She rested her hand along his jaw, then spun on her heel to race to her vehicle. True to his word, Jefferson laid down on the floor of the back seat while she drove to the location, praying they would be in time.

Four miles out of town, the GPS directed her to turn onto a dirt road lined by trees. The vehicle jounced over the ruts, eliciting a groan from Jefferson. "Sorry." The road abruptly ended in a small clearing. No other vehicles were visible, but the automated voice directed her to continue straight. "I have to walk the rest of the way."

Without waiting for a reply, she parked and cut the engine before leaving the car. She spotted a faint path ahead of her and sprinted down the narrow lane. Branches slapped at her face and clawed at her hair, but she ignored the scratches and tugs, her only thought on getting Ethan. The disembodied GPS voice announced she had arrived seconds before she saw a dilapidated shack in front of her. Vines intertwined with the weathered wood. The door hung on one hinge, and the busted windowpanes grinned like a first grader with missing front teeth.

"Ethan?"

A muffled sound from inside the shack drew her toward the door. Then a stocky figure clad in black from head to toe appeared in the doorway. Eve swallowed a scream and squared her shoulders. This wasn't one of the men who had attempted to snatch Ethan from his home, so she surmised he was the mastermind.

The man slid back his sleeve and glanced at an Apple

watch. "Right on time. I must say, I'm impressed. Usually doctors make you wait."

The cultured tones did little to alter the man's thuggish manner. "Where's Ethan?"

"Oh, he's inside with a friend." The man's eyes crinkled as if smiling behind the black facemask. "Although friend is not quite accurate. Employee is better but doesn't sound as nice. My second friend tells me you came alone. Bravo for following directions."

A muscular man stepped from the woods. "Boss."

"I told you to keep an eye on her vehicle." The bossman's snarl did little to alter the other man's demeanor.

He shrugged. "I watched it for five minutes, then took a look inside. No one there."

Eve prayed her face wouldn't give away her delight that Jefferson had somehow managed to get out of her vehicle without the man noticing. *Please, God. Let him stay safe!* Time to find out who this boss was and where her son was. "Where's Ethan?"

"The brat is fine." Bossman's eyes glittered above his facemask. "For now. He'll stay safe as long as you cooperate."

"What do you want?" But she already knew—her signature on the document renouncing her right to the Brandt estate. Maybe it would throw Bossman off his game if she told him. "You know my signature under duress won't stand up in court."

His eyes widened a fraction before narrowing. "It won't ever come to court."

The cold menace behind the words frightened Eve, but she schooled her expression to show mild interest. "You sound pretty confident." She tapped her finger against her cheek. "But you can't hide behind that ridiculous facemask forever." The man snorted, but she caught a flicker of fear in his dark eyes. "You won't get away with it."

"I have and I will." He nodded once, and the muscular man grabbed her arm in a punishing grip.

Eve bit back a yelp and allowed herself to be yanked into the shack. Inside, it wasn't as dark as she'd feared because of the broken or missing slats constituting the structure's sides. The roof also had a huge hole on the backside, allowing sunlight to stream in. She swept her gaze around the dust-encrusted floor, desperate to find her son. A small bundle of clothes against the far wall moved slightly, and Ethan's white face peered at her.

"Dr. Eve!" The little boy stumbled to his feet, but Bossman intercepted him.

"Not so fast. Dr. Eve has some signing to do first."

He manhandled her over to a wooden crate and thrust her onto it. "Stay."

She bristled at his command—she was no dog—but Ethan's safety came before her feelings, so she swallowed her anger. She would be compliant until she could figure out a way to escape with her son. Bossman shoved Ethan back into the corner. The boy fell with a cry that had Eve's muscles tensing. But Ethan righted himself, rubbing his elbow and locking his gaze on her.

"How are you doing, Ethan?" She strove for a conversational tone to calm his fears.

"O-o-k-k-a-y." The drawn out reply concerned her. "C-o-o-l-l-d."

The shack, although far from sheltering them from the elements, held some of the sun's warmth. "He's not doing well. I think he might be in shock."

Bossman carried a folder over to her. "Then you'd best sign these papers."

The spark of elation in the man's eyes as he handed her the folder and a pen made her uncomfortable, as did the fact she didn't know where the other kidnapper was. She also didn't trust Bossman because her only reason for being alive was he needed her signature. If she refused to sign, she feared he might hurt Ethan. Maybe if she stalled, Jefferson would arrive with the cavalry. One glance at Ethan's shivering body sealed her decision.

After flipping open the folder, she stared down at the papers, not reading them but organizing her thoughts. She would have one chance to distract Bossman, so she needed to be on her A game. Bossman's lack of concern about Ethan's condition fueled her fury, drove her to put into words what had been circling her brain during the drive here. "So which cousin are you?"

JEFFERSON SKIRTED THE SHACK IN A WIDE BERTH, KEEPING WELL back in the woods to hide his movements. Thank goodness he had managed to slip out of the vehicle on the opposite side when Eve got out, shutting his door in synch with hers. A tangle of vines allowed him to camouflage himself quickly while she jogged to the path. Only a few minutes passed before a beefy man came out of the woods and approached her rental. The man studied the vehicle, then walked around it before coming closer to peer into the windows. In his hiding place behind thick foliage, Jefferson caught a glimpse of a weapon under the man's jacket. He let out his breath when the man went in the same direction as Eve had gone without discovering his hiding place.

Once certain no one else was watching the clearing, Jefferson sent his location to Detective Cunningham, along with the info about the armed man, who matched the description of one of the kidnappers. Then he worked his way free of the vines and went after Eve, but through the woods to avoid running into anyone. Good thing he was wearing jeans and a long-sleeved t-shirt, as the branches and thorns tugged at his clothing.

Soon he spotted an abandoned structure through a gap in the trees. He crept closer, then crouched behind a fallen log. He couldn't see much but listened hard. The muffled sounds of voices reached his ears. He needed to be a little closer to hear the words. His phone vibrated in his pocket, and he silenced it without looking. He couldn't chance someone noticing a reflection and finding him.

The voices faded even more. Jefferson counted to thirty, then eased to his full height. Maybe if he went around to the back of the shack, he might find a more hidden approach. He sent up a prayer his movements wouldn't be heard or seen and started his journey.

Jefferson breathed a prayer of thanksgiving as he noted the building's lack of windows along the back. He moved closer, taking care to avoid sticks and dried leaves. Still within the shelter of the woods, he eyed the shack to see where he could enter. While some of the boards were loose, they were vertical and thus not able to admit him into the building. He leaned to the left to see that side of the building. Aha! A door nearly blended into the weathered wood. Perhaps those inside weren't even aware of its existence, given its location on the side rather than back. Perfect.

He decided to chance checking his phone, hoping Cunningham had been the one texting. Relief poured over him at her message:

Will be there in less than 10 min. Do not attempt a rescue on your own.

He ignored her command and sent her an update.

Kidnappers and Eve in shack. Going to check to see if Ethan's inside too. Turning off phone.

He powered it down, not wanting any noise to give him away and stepped out of the woods. No movement outside the shack. He sidled up to the door and placed his ear against the flecking wood in time to hear Eve ask which cousin someone was.

"What?" A man's unfamiliar voice blustered, but even Jefferson could hear the man was rattled by her question. "I don't know what you're talking about."

"Sure you do." Eve's confident tone rang out loud and clear. "You're greedy, wanting all of Owen Brandt's money—or at least more of it than your share—for yourself. You must be pretty desperate to stoop to kidnapping a child and threatening me."

"We wouldn't be here if Donahue had convinced you to sign those papers years ago, but you left as soon as you turned eighteen and refused all contact."

"Why am I not surprised my supposed uncle was in cahoots with the likes of you. For money, I suppose."

"Yeah, five million dollars is a lot of dough to make sure someone disappeared forever. Or at least until they turned twenty-five."

Jefferson winced as another piece to the puzzle fell into place—Donahue's involvement in keeping Eve away from her paternal grandparents for the life insurance money.

"Twenty-five."

Keep them talking, Eve, Jefferson silently urged. *You're doing a great job so far!*

"I bet it has to do with a trust, one that would revert to the family money pot if unclaimed or renounced by my twenty-fifth birthday." Her voice hardened. "How much did you promise Donahue?"

"Too much, and he still couldn't close the deal. Now enough talking. Sign the documents."

Ethan cried out, his son's voice high pitched and frightened. "Let me go!"

"Sign it—or say goodbye to your son."

CHAPTER

SEVENTEEN

Eve bit back her own scream as Bossman's hand closed around Ethan's throat. "Okay, I'll sign the papers." She dropped the pen. The man growled more threats as she felt around on the ground for the writing instrument. Her fingers closed around it and something slim and heavy. She managed to drag the object toward her along with the pen, placing her foot on top of the unknown item.

"Where do I sign?" She fluttered the papers as if trying to figure out where to affix her signature.

"Take him." Bossman shoved Ethan in the direction of the muscular man, who hauled the kid up by the scruff of his T-shirt.

Tears streamed down her son's face, but Eve steeled herself to ignore them. She had to concentrate on neutralizing the threat so her son would be safe. To do that, she would pretend to cooperate.

Bossman snatched the papers from her and shuffled them. "Here." He pointed to a line.

She braced the paper on top of the manila folder but try as she might, she couldn't get the ink to exit the pen. "It's not working."

He blew out a breath, then grabbed the pen from her fingers. "You'd better not be playing with me." But his attempts to write with the pen on the back of the folder didn't produce any visible line. He stalked over to the other man, giving Eve time to investigate what she'd found. An old railroad spike, its black lead a little rusty. With Bossman's back turned and his body shielding her from the other man's view, she hefted it up and concealed it under her thigh. With enough force, she could incapacitate Bossman. That still left the muscleman, but maybe with the boss out of commission, he wouldn't hurt Ethan.

Her head pounded. Stress and fear tightened the muscles in her body. Eve wrapped her fingers around the pointed end of the spike, intending to use the larger, square head as a weapon. In her mind's eye, she reviewed the best possible place on Bossman's head to incapacitate him without causing permanent damage—or death. Despite his actions, she did not want to kill him. If she could hit him behind his ear, she should be able to knock him out, at least according to advice she recalled from a fellow resident who boxed for exercise.

Bossman returned with another pen, cutting short her planning time. "This one works." He tossed the pen onto her lap, then leaned over with the folder and papers in his hand.

Here was her chance. Eve swung the spike toward the side of Bossman's head, aiming for the space behind his left ear. It connected with a sickening crack, sending the man wheeling back and down.

Wood splintered as Jefferson charged into the shack from the far corner. His gaze met Eve's, then he nodded toward the man hauling a squirming Ethan outside. "Secure him." He pointed to Bossman as he raced past. "I'll get our son."

His words warmed her heart as she hastened to the still figure lying on the dusty floor. She crouched beside him to check his pulse at the neck. The steady beat reassured her she had been successful in knocking him out without ending his life. Blood trickled from the wound behind his ear, but she ignored that as she patted him down to find the gun she'd seen him holding earlier.

There! She pulled the weapon from the pocket of his jacket and tossed it into the far-left corner of the shack, then she raced outside to see Jefferson squared off with the muscular man, who held a white-faced Ethan in front of him like a shield with his handgun pointed at the boy's temple. A long, angry abrasion across the left side of Ethan's face pushed her rage toward the surface, but she tamped it down. She could be furious later. For now, she needed to help her son through the next few minutes.

"It's over. Let him go." Jefferson didn't acknowledge her as she stepped to his side, keeping his attention on the man holding Ethan.

"Stay back or else." The menace in the other man's tone made Eve suppress a shudder.

Eve focused on Ethan, whose wide eyes and shaking body told her he was going into shock. She needed to help him calm down. "Hey, Ethan."

No response. She moved directly into his line of sight and dropped to her knees to bring herself to his eye level. "Ethan, sweetie."

This time, his gaze snagged hers and held. She curved her lips into a smile. "Hi, there."

"Hiiii, Dr.," he swallowed hard, "Eve."

Good, he recognized her. Jefferson continued talking to the man holding the gun to Ethan's head, but Eve tuned out their conversation. "It's been a pretty scary day, hasn't it?"

Ethan's shoulders slumped. "Yeah. I wanna go home."

"Me too." She paused. "I bet Willoughby will be glad to see us both. I've been neglecting him lately."

At the mention of her cat, Ethan attempted a smile. "He's funny, with his droopy ear."

"He is." She racked her brain for an anecdote about the cat

to take Ethan's mind off the current situation. Ah, yes. The mac and cheese disaster would do nicely. "Do you remember how I locked him up when we ate mac and cheese?"

"Yeah, but I thought that was because your window was busted."

Great, probably shouldn't have reminded him of that but she went on. "That was part of it, but mostly it was because he loves mac and cheese."

Her son's eyes grew even larger. "He does?"

"Yep. One day shortly after I adopted him—or he adopted me—I had made some mac and cheese but had to sign for a delivery package and left my bowl on the counter. When I returned, Willoughby had helped himself to my dinner."

"Wow."

"He'd eaten nearly half the bowl, so I have to put him in another room whenever I make it." Behind the armed man, Eve noted uniformed police and deputies approaching with weapons drawn. She winged a prayer for the safe ending of the standoff and schooled her face to avoid tipping off the man.

"Please release my son. The police will be here soon." Jefferson didn't betray what he must have seen as well. "You haven't hurt anyone yet."

The man's hand holding the gun to Ethan's temple wavered, and Eve prayed the man would listen to Jefferson. Then he dropped his arm, lowering the gun, and released his grip on Ethan's arm.

"Ethan, come to me, slowly," Eve commanded, wanting Ethan away from the man before the kidnapper realized he was surrounded.

Her son walked toward her a few steps, then stumbled into a run. She grabbed him but kept her attention on the armed man.

"Put the gun down." Jefferson's voice sounded calm, causal even.

The man wavered a second, then bent to place the weapon on the ground. As soon as he'd done so, the command, "Police, freeze!" rang in the air.

The man raised his hands above his head as uniformed officers and deputies poured into the clearing. It was over, and Eve turned her full attention to her trembling son.

"Are you okay?" She cradled a sobbing Ethan against her, careful not to hold him too tight until she could assess his injuries.

"Ethan!" Jefferson swooped in to wrap the two of them in his arms. Together, they sat in a cocoon of love while law enforcement personnel cuffed the muscular man and attended to Bossman in the shack.

Over Ethan's head, Eve noticed a tall man in handcuffs at the edge of the clearing, and she breathed out thanks for the capture of the third man.

"Clear!" The word echoed as more voices informed them police had secured the scene.

"Hey, we're safe now." She brushed a hand over his head. "Jefferson, I should check Ethan."

"Of course." Jefferson loosened his hold and rocked back on his heels.

"Ethan, sweetie, let me take a look at you, okay?" She gently probed his limbs, running her hands lightly over his midsection. Dirt and leaves in his hair attested to his journey through the woods. A few red scratches on his arms had already crusted over, but beyond the abrasion on his cheek, he appeared unharmed. "What hurts?"

"My face." He swiped at his nose with the back of his hand, leaving another streak of dirt on his face. "The bad man hit me when I wouldn't stop crying."

"The one who..." She wasn't sure how to describe Bossman.

"The one who wanted you to sign something." Tears

pooled in his eyes again. "I heard him tell the other man he wasn't going to share with a brat."

She drew him close, rocking him back and forth in her arms. "Shh. It's over—all the bad men are caught." *Lord, please let it be so!*

"I want my dad." Ethan's words seared across her heart. Of course he wanted Jefferson. He had no idea his mother was holding him close. She let go, and Jefferson swung Ethan up into his arms. The boy wrapped his legs around his father's middle and buried his head in his shoulder as more sobs shook his small body.

Eve sucked in a breath, then let it out in a whoosh of air as her own tears streamed down her cheeks, relief at the apprehension of the men involved in the kidnapping attempts and assaults. Soon they would have answers to their many questions, but for now, she would be content to bask in the safe return of her son.

JEFFERSON TIPTOED DOWNSTAIRS, PRAYING ETHAN WOULD STAY asleep this time. He'd been up and down the stairs three times since settling his son in bed for the night. Each time Ethan had screamed from a night terror, his heart rate had skyrocketed. But the boy had been alone in his room, shivering and sobbing from half-remembered nightmares related to his earlier ordeal.

Eve had gone to the hospital to check on Donahue, taking Cunningham with her to question the man who had been involved in a scheme to disinherit Eve since he'd gotten custody after the death of her parents. He prayed she would find the answers she sought, especially the one that had her fearing the car wreck that had taken her mom and dad hadn't been an accident. He checked his phone, relieved to find a text from her saying she was on her way home.

He rubbed his chin, his beard rough under the pads of his fingers. He dropped onto the couch, propping up his legs. Willoughby bounded up and settled on his lap, his steady purr as Jefferson stroked the soft fur soothing after the stresses of the day. Once more, he gave thanks to God for bringing Ethan home safe and for catching the men responsible for the assaults and kidnapping. While Ethan took a bath after an early supper, Cunningham had told them both the two hired guns pointed the finger at Bossman as the one who had hired them and devised the kidnapping schemes. Both had denied setting Eve's cabin on fire, but the muscular one—a thug with a long record called Davey Grossman—confessed to the brick through her window. The taller one—another repeat offender named Steve Wyndham—had been behind the kidnapping attempts on the path and at the nature center.

The mastermind had yet to reveal his name, with both henchman vowing they had no idea what it might be, so Cunningham suggested a visit to Donahue might fill in some of the blanks while Bossman awaited his attorney. The man had the audacity to vow he would sue Eve for administering the lump on his head, but Cunningham didn't appear too worried about that, given the physical evidence backing up Eve's tale of coercion and the accomplices' stories of his illegal instructions.

Jefferson closed his eyes. *Thank you, Lord, for your protection today. Please let my son sleep and not be plagued by any more nightmares. Give us wisdom in how to tell Ethan she's his mother. Prepare both of their hearts for this new connection and journey together.*

Eve's beauty had shone through today despite the stress, fatigue, and tear tracks on her cheeks. Who was he kidding? He always thought she was gorgeous. Seeing her again on the path with Ethan only days ago had reignited his feelings for her, but he hadn't wanted to face the truth then. Now he wouldn't fight it any longer. He loved her, had always loved her. The love from their teenage romance had blossomed into a love for a lifetime. The seeds planted during their senior year of high school had lain dormant like a bulb during the harsh winter months. He could only hope he would get the opportunity to see it bloom again.

And God? I would really love a second chance with Eve.

"Jefferson?"

Jefferson pried his eyes open as the scent of rosemary drifted over him. Eve scratched Willoughby's head as the cat stretched on Jefferson's lap.

He muffled a yawn. "I must have fallen asleep. What time is it?"

"Eight-thirty."

The cat jumped off his lap and stalked out of the room, tail held high. "I thought we were friends."

Eve chuckled, the sound tugging an answering smile to his own lips. "He doesn't like to have his rest disturbed."

Jefferson swung his legs to the floor to make room on the couch for Eve to join him. "How did it go?"

She flopped down beside him, kicking off her shoes. "Draining." She leaned her head back against the cushions. "But insightful."

He surveyed the tired line of her body. "You're exhausted."

"I am." She let out a slow sigh. "How's Ethan?"

"He's woken up three times with nightmares."

She grimaced. "Poor kid."

"Yeah." He rotated his shoulders to ease some of the stiffness from napping on the sofa. "I scoped out a child therapist in this area, as I wanted to have someone in mind if he needed it. He saw one in Boston after George died."

"That's good. Cunningham did say she had been in touch with the Boston PD about George's car accident since Ethan was supposed to be in the vehicle with him."

Jefferson's heart hitched at the thought the unnamed man might have been responsible for his twin's death.

"They finally have a name for the man—Clark Brandt. He's the oldest son of the second wife."

"So we were right that this has to do with Owen Brandt's will."

"Yep." She sighed again. "It all boiled down to money and greed."

He reached for her hand, interlacing his fingers through hers. "It's over now. Ethan's safe. You're safe."

"But we'll be picking apart this mess for a while longer." She turned toward him, pain shimmering in her brown eyes. "Donahue confessed to sabotaging my parents' vehicle. He and Clark have been scheming to get their hands on my grandfather's money for years. Donahue, using his connections to the Irish mob, was supposed to be my guardian and keep me away from that side of the family until after my twenty-fifth birthday. In exchange, Clark would make sure Donahue got the $5 million insurance money. I'm not sure how he hid my existence from my grandfather given the insurance payout, but Donahue said my grandfather was pretty cut up about the death of his oldest son and probably didn't look too closely into the finances. Owen Brandt had set up a trust for me, as he had all his grandchildren, and couldn't simply dissolve it even though he thought I was dead. It would revert to the family pot, so to speak, once I turned twenty-five and remained dead, which is why Clark was desperate to have me sign the disinheritance papers for me and on behalf of Ethan too."

He settled back on the couch and drew her into his arms. "I'm so sorry you didn't get a chance to know your grandfather."

"Me too."

"I suppose your grandfather's death triggered everything?"

"I think so." She snuggled closer, her head on his shoulder. "Unbeknownst to the family, Owen Brandt had started investigating my parents' crash. He'd apparently learned I wasn't dead and had traced me to the Donahues in Boston. Cunningham learned this from a lawyer working for the estate. The one we spoke to was in cahoots with Clark and helping him fix it so the trust money would revert to the family."

"It's terrible what greed will do to a person."

"Indeed." She smothered a yawn, and he decided to table his remaining questions in favor of enjoying the quiet of being with the woman he loved.

Jefferson shifted into a more comfortable position in which to hold her close, then dropped a light kiss on the top of her head. Her body relaxed against his. He decided to enjoy the moment a little longer and allowed himself to close his eyes. His last thought before sleep claimed him again was how he wanted to hold Eve like this for the rest of his life.

EIGHTEEN

"Aaahhh."

Eve jolted awake at the sound of Ethan's cry. She lay on the couch, a light blanket tossed over her. Willoughby meowed his displeasure at being dislodged as she pushed the cat off her lap. No sound besides Ethan's whimpers and the cat's meows greeted her ears. No time to worry about where Jefferson was, so she dashed up the stairs to Ethan's room.

Ethan cried out again, and she eased his door open more. Her son lay tangled in his sheet and blanket, thrashing about in the throes of a nightmare. The grey light filtering in through the open curtains told her it was nearly morning.

She approached his bed and sat on the edge, away from his flaying arms. She began singing a soft lullaby, one she thought her mother must have sung to her as she knew Lorraine had never done so. But the words had always stayed with her. "'Hush, little baby, don't say a word, momma's gonna buy you a mockingbird.'"

Ethan's movements slowed.

"'If that mockingbird won't sing, momma's gonna buy you a diamond ring.'" She smoothed back his hair from his forehead as his body stilled. "'If that diamond ring turns glass, momma's gonna buy you a looking glass.'"

His eyes flickered open and his gaze fastened on her face. "Momma?"

She couldn't deny him, not in this moment, not when it was the truth. "Yes, Ethan?"

"You're here." The words breathed out of him like a prayer, and he threw his arms around her neck. "I knew you'd come. I prayed and prayed and prayed so long for a momma. My first dad told me you would come one day. He said you always loved me but had to leave for a little while but that you'd be back when God said it was the right time." He pulled back, his hands leaving her neck to frame her face. "It's time, isn't it?"

"Yes, my darling boy. It's time." She kissed his hands, then his cheek, her tears mingling with his. "It's the perfect time."

"Oh, Momma." He hugged her again. "I knew God would answer my prayer when I saw the way Dad looked at you."

Eve's heart nearly burst with happiness, then his last statement penetrated the haze of joy. "What do you mean?"

Ethan snuggled into her side, leaning against her. "Dad likes you. More than likes you, I think, but I'm only eight, so I don't really understand all the grownup stuff. My first dad told me all about how you and my second dad used to love each other when you were young, and how that kind of love didn't leave your heart. Kind of like the love of a mom for her kids, he said. That's why he was sure you were loving me even though you weren't here with us."

Eve sorted through what he said, grateful for George's preparation of Ethan's heart for this reunion. "Yes, I always loved you, even when we were apart, and I'm glad we don't have to be apart any longer."

Ethan pulled back, his eyes shining. "Then you'll be my momma now?"

She swiped the moisture from her cheeks. "Yes." She

remembered her charred cabin. "Although I will need a new place to stay since it will be a while before I can live in my cabin again."

His eyes filled with tears and his lips wobbled. "You're not staying here with us?"

Oh, she so didn't want to break his little heart, but while she and Jefferson had shared that amazing kiss, she wasn't sure he had completely forgiven her for the past. She hoped with time, he would be ready to move forward. "My staying here was only supposed to be temporary."

"Dad!" Ethan wiggled out of bed.

Eve's cheeks heated as she wondered how much Jefferson had overheard as she twisted to see him stooping to hug his son. He wore running clothes with a fluorescent yellow safety harness.

"Eww, you're sweaty." Ethan scrunched up his face. "And smelly."

Jefferson grinned. "You're the one who wanted a hug."

"Don't remind me." Ethan edged farther away from his father, giving him a wide berth as he scrambled back into bed. "Guess what, Dad! Dr. Eve is my mother."

"I know." Jefferson lounged in the doorway, his body backlit by the hall light. "What do you think about that?"

Eve couldn't see his expression, so she wasn't sure what Jefferson thought about her revealing her status to Ethan without telling Jefferson first.

"It's cool." Ethan swiveled his head from Eve to Jefferson. "But you know what would be even more cool?"

"I can't imagine anything being more cool than gaining a mother," Jefferson said.

Her son rolled his eyes. "Grownups can be so dense."

Eve burst out laughing, and Jefferson quirked his lips into a smile.

Ethan pointed at his dad. "You like her." Then he directed his index finger at Eve. "And you like him."

She tilted her head to glance at Jefferson, who had straightened. Their gazes locked, and heat of a different kind warmed her body.

"So why can't she stay with us?"

Ethan's question bounced around the room that seemed to shrink with each step Jefferson took toward Eve.

"Why not indeed?" His soft question sent a thrill through her. He held out his hand, and she placed hers in his slightly sweaty grasp as she rose to her feet.

A whiff of outdoors and male sweat wafted over her, but she wasn't as turned off as Ethan had been. "Several reasons come to mind."

"Such as?" He raised his eyebrows and widened his eyes in a comical expression of wonder.

"Willoughby, for starters."

"I think the cat has already made himself at home." Jefferson eased closer, allowing her a glimpse of the longing in his eyes. His thumb made circles on the back of her hand.

Her heart rate galloped into high gear.

"I love Willoughby!" Ethan's shout tugged a smile to her lips.

"Good to know." She licked her dry lips and nearly gasped at the passion flaring in Jefferson's gaze. "Then there's the issue of not being asked."

"Ask her, Dad. Ask her," Ethan chanted, the bed creaking from his bouncing.

Eve choked back a laugh at Ethan's enthusiasm and decided to tease Jefferson a little. With a hand on her hip, she cocked her head. "Well, Mr. Smith? Do you have something you want to ask me?"

"I do, Dr. Davenport." Jefferson leaned closer, putting his lips next to her ear. "Will you make me the happiest man by consenting to be my wife?"

Despite expecting the proposal, his words washed out the

hurt and sorrow of the past and brought in the sweetness and hope of the future.

"Momma, say yes!"

Eve glanced over her shoulder at her son, who nodded vigorously in return. She turned back to meet Jefferson's warm gaze. "I guess I shouldn't disappoint our son."

He lowered his head to hover his mouth inches from hers. "You're not worried about disappointing me?"

She shook her head. "Never." She feathered a gentle kiss on his lips. "I will marry you."

"Yay! We'll be a real family!" Ethan cheered again, then bounded out of bed. "I'm going to tell Willoughby he can stay."

He scampered out of the room, leaving Eve and Jefferson alone.

"He's going to be a handful, isn't he?" She raised her face to her new fiancé's.

"Are you up to it?" He cupped her cheek with his hand.

"I am as long as I have you by my side." His answering kiss promised her the world and then some. Eve returned his kiss with all the love in her heart, thankful for God's kind providence in restoring what had been lost and building an even better future for her than she had ever imagined.

THE END

Now a sneak peek at the first chapter in Fatal Recall, *book two in* Twin Oaks Secrets, *coming summer of 2026.*

Nola Johnson exited the city bus, her golden collie at her heels. "Out, Molly." The dog, a mix of golden retriever and border collie, obediently hopped out onto the pavement, her bright yellow "Therapy Dog" vest catching the morning sun. She waved to the bus driver, then paused outside the entrance to the Twin Oaks Public Library. Her heart hammered, and she took several deep cleansing breaths. She could do this. She'd done it a million times, but that was before a car accident had totaled her vehicle and left her with gaps in her memory. The doctor had assured her the condition—selective amnesia—would likely resolve itself over time. But then, he didn't have to live with no memories of the past few weeks, while also not knowing if she'd be able to recall particular events or information.

Molly nudged her leg. "You're right. I need to stop worrying. It was an accident." She patted the canine's head, but the sense of unease refused to leave her. Even as she reassured the canine, the sensation of being watched shot through her, sending her adrenaline into the stratosphere. A quick look around showed no one out of place, but the feeling someone was watching her had become more pronounced in the last few days. She didn't think she'd experienced the fissures of fear snaking down her spine before the accident, but now she often battled the sense someone was spying on her with malevolent intent—which was silly. In her late forties, she'd become a person most people didn't even notice.

Molly moved beside her, her body wiggling as more children entered the library. Right. She and Molly had a job to do, so they'd better get to it. "Let's get going so we're not late for story time."

As they approached the automatic doors, she shivered as

if a cold breeze had washed over her instead of the mild October air. Probably her senses were heightened because of last night's nightmare. A shadowy figure had chased her around a dark building, trapping her in the stairwell. She'd awaken before the person had reached her, but even in the light of a bright morning, she couldn't shake the anxiety. As if sensing her discomfort, Molly licked her hand.

"I'm just being silly this morning, girl." She scratched the rescue dog between the ears. "Don't worry—we'll be okay." Nola squared her shoulders as they entered the library's lobby before veering right into the children's section. She had spent years taking care of her reclusive parents, leaving her with little life experience. But since their deaths a little over five years ago, she had slowly built a new life for herself in a new place away from the bullying of the past.

Sean Kingsley with his terrier mix, Lincoln, had settled into their usual spot against the wall. She waved at him and took Molly to the opposite corner, positioning her back against a shelf. At her command, Molly lay down. She loved bringing Molly to the library so kids could practice their reading. In the five years since she'd moved to Twin Oaks, she'd found a real community and a sense of purpose as she trained therapy dogs for Happy Sunshine Farm, which offered horse and other forms of animal therapy to both children and adults with special needs or disabilities. Farm owner Rose Johnson had taken her under her wing when she'd arrived in town, ready for a fresh start. Working with animals had provided a way to heal and blossom into her own person.

Nola shook her head, dispelling the memories both good and bad of her more than twenty years of servitude in her parents' house. She rubbed her forehead as the beginnings of a headache inched along the base of her skull. Maybe drinking more of her coffee, secured in a travel mug, would help. If not, she'd take some ibuprofen, although she avoided medications, even the over-the-counter ones, as much as possible. Her hypochondriac parents had taken every kind of medications, supplements, and herbal remedies they could to dubious effect. The doctor had told her to expect headaches from the bump on her head she'd sustained during the car accident, but to come see him again if over-the-counter pain relievers didn't alleviate the pain.

Molly pressed against her leg as two children stopped in front of the dog. "Hello." Glad for the distraction, Nola smiled at the pair.

"What's your dog's name?" A boy of about six clutched the hand of a younger girl.

"Molly. What's yours?"

"I'm Will and this is Sandy." Will never took his attention off Molly.

Part of her job was to guide the children into safe interactions with Molly. "Hold out your hand so she can give it a good sniff."

"Like this?" The boy stretched out his hand toward Molly's head. The dog licked it, triggering giggles from both children.

"Now you can pet her."

Both kids dropped to their knees beside Molly, petting her and whispering to each other. After a few minutes, Nola interrupted. "Molly is a therapy dog—she's trained to listen while you practice your reading out loud. Would you like to pick a book to read to her?"

Will's eyes widened, delight spreading a smile across his thin face. "That would be awesome."

Sandy, who Nola supposed was his sister, given their similar coloring and eyes, plopped down crisscross in front of Molly. "I'm waiting here."

Her brother frowned. "Mom said to stay with me."

"Molly and I will keep an eye on her while you grab a book," Nola offered.

That seemed to satisfy Will because he scampered off into

the stacks in search of a book. Nola took the opportunity to sip more coffee, placing the mug behind her on an upper shelf out of the way. The boy returned with an Elephant and Piggy book by Moe Williams, which he read slowly to Molly. When he'd finished, his mother came and thanked Nola and Molly before leading the siblings away. Molly returned to her waiting poise.

Nola's headache hadn't dissipated, even with more coffee. She rummaged in her backpack for her small bottle of over-the-counter medicines and downed two ibuprofen tablets with another sip of coffee. She put the mug back on the shelf. Nola surveyed the kids and parents milling about, some reading and others pursuing the shelves. Sean had a small group of kids around Lincoln, one of which read the terrier a Curious George book. Then a girl who Nola judged to be about eight approached them.

"Does your dog really like stories?" She clasped a stack of books to her chest, her tone skeptical.

Nola shrugged, as if she didn't know Molly loved to listen to kids. "Why don't you ask her?"

The child's eyes widened. "Will she answer?"

"You won't know until you ask Molly." This was Nola's favorite part of the job—helping a child overcome reluctance to engage with Molly.

The girl considered Molly for a long moment, then said, "Molly, do you like stories?"

Molly woofed softly, drawing a delighted smile from the girl, who promptly sat beside the dog and opened a book. While she listened to *The Korean Cinderella*, one of the many iterations of the popular fairy tale, Nola again felt a prickling sensation at the back of her neck. Someone was watching her. With ill intent. That much was clear to her, although she couldn't have said for sure why she'd concluded that. The menace from her nightmare returned, filling her with the need to leave. Now.

She surreptitiously glanced around the children's nook at the patrons to see if she could spot what had triggered her flight response. The crowd appeared the same as most Saturdays. As the girl started on her second book—this one about a Mexican princess—Nola's gaze landed on a tall man with muscular arms a few years older than her stationed at the edge of the children's area.

Her heart pounded as her eyes collided with his slate gray ones, a perfect complement to his salt-and-pepper hair. Shock reverberated through her as recognition nipped at her memory. She'd seen him recently. She broke eye contact as she struggled to bring up the context. Then she had it—she'd seen him at the park yesterday when she'd taken Molly for her afternoon walk. Another memory surfaced. The same man had been a couple of lines over at the grocery store a few days earlier. Twin Oaks wasn't a big town, so seeing a stranger three times in as many days meant one of two things—either he was a new resident or he'd been following her. Her stomach flip-flopped, making her regret the pancake breakfast she'd consumed at the Twin Oaks Diner prior to coming to the library. The pressure in her head increased as she struggled to concentrate on the girl's reading to Molly and not on the stranger whose intense gaze troubled her.

Her knee jiggled, drawing Molly's attention away from the young reader. The dog snuffled, pushing her wet nose against Nola's leg. The desire to leave the library overwhelmed her, as the invisible compression band encircling her head tightened. She didn't question her instinct to bolt but instead curbed it. Better to leave quietly and naturally, as if she'd always planned to exit story time early.

The girl finished the book and reached for another one. Nola forestalled her. "Molly needs a break, so maybe we'll see you next week?"

The child's eyes lit up. "You're here every Saturday?"

"We are."

The girl patted Molly on the head as Nola stood with the dog's leash in hand. She shouldered the backpack, then bent to grab her travel mug. Her hand slipped slightly on the smooth outside, but she managed to hold onto it, cupping her palm around the mug. She waved goodbye to Sean and Lincoln, and headed to the exit with Molly at her heels. Outside the library, she drained the rest of her coffee, then secured the beverage container in the outside mesh holder of her backpack. The Next Bus app indicated her ride would arrive in less than five minutes. Not ideal, but until she could sort out the insurance with her carrier, she had to wait to get new wheels. At least the city had a robust bus system but she missed her dark blue crossover.

Molly bumped against her leg as Nola surveyed her surroundings again but didn't see the man from the library. His direct gaze had disconcerted her, since she rarely attracted male attention. She stifled a sense of longing for a family of her own. Her time for love had passed her by as she'd concentrated on caring for her much-older parents. No sense playing the what-if game with handsome strangers in mind.

The pavement shifted under her feet and she stumbled into Molly. No, that couldn't be right. Sidewalks didn't move, but this one seemed to be, making it difficult for her to remain on her feet. Her tongue rested heavy in her mouth, an early sign of anaphylactic shock. But how could she have come in contact with peanuts? The children who'd read to Molly hadn't had sticky hands—she kept baby wipes in her backpack in case she suspected a child might have snacked on a PB&J before story time.

Breathing became more difficult as her tongue swelled, filling her mouth and constricting her air supply. Panic beat at the door in her mind, but she refused to give in. Her EpiPen. Her brain grew fuzzier as she struggled to remember where the life-saving medicine was. Her backpack. Outside pocket.

With herculean effort, Nola slipped the bag off her shoulders, swaying as the loss of the weight nearly overbalanced her. The bag thumped to the brick sidewalk. When she reached down for the zipper, she couldn't stop her body from continuing the downward motion. She smacked onto the bricks, her palms and knees bearing the brunt of her collapse. Molly barked, tension swirling in her wiggling body. Nola reached out a hand to her dog but couldn't complete the gesture before fighting for breath took over every instinct. *Please God, send help!*

PATTERSON MARLOWE HELD HANDS WITH HIS SEVEN-YEAR-OLD niece, Hailey, as her five-year-old brother, Davey, skipped ahead to trigger the automatic doors to exit the library. The kids had been disappointed the woman with the therapy dog had left before the end of the advertised story time. Both children had decided her dog looked more approachable than the smaller one the man had. Patterson may or may not have gently pushed them in that direction. He'd always preferred larger animals than yippy ones like the terrier. Although, to be fair, the little dog hadn't uttered a single yap while "listening" to children read to him.

As the trio left the library, the woman with the dog waited near the bus stop. She wavered as if having trouble keeping her balance, then shrugged off her backpack. When she bent down, she fell over, landing on her side on the sidewalk.

Patterson was by her side in an instant, his instincts propelling him forward. Kneeling beside her, he studied her to see what had caused her collapse. Her face had turned a splotchy red. Her breaths came in ragged gasps, her brown eyes huge.

"Is she okay, Uncle Patterson?" Hailey's question reminded him of his duty to the kids but he couldn't leave the woman lying there on the sidewalk in such obvious medical distress.

"I'm going to help her." Patterson nodded toward a bench next to the library's entrance. "Wait there with your brother."

As Hailey grabbed her sibling's hand and dragged him over to the bench against his protests, Patterson turned his attention back to the woman. "I'm Patterson. Okay if I help you?"

She nodded and wheezed out, "Nola." Her lips lost more of their color, indicating her struggle to breath. Her symptoms reminded him of anaphylactic shock, which he'd seen up close and personnel in the Army's Special Forces when one of his privates had accidentally ingested a piece of shrimp in a bowl of fish stew.

"I think you're having an allergic reaction to something."

She moved her hand toward the pack and mouthed what he thought was "EpiPen." Her dog whined, then poked her nose at the bag. Patterson opened the main compartment but the canine growled and nudged the bag again.

"Not there?" He unzipped the outside compartment and spotted the EpiPen. "Got it." He removed the blue plastic tip and jammed the device into the woman's thigh. He depressed the plunger, waited to hear the click, then counted to five before releasing it.

"Hey, man, is she okay?" A man with a baby strapped to his chest in a carrier paused beside him.

"Not sure. Would you call 911 for me?" Patterson returned his attention to Nola, whose breathing eased a little as the red splotches on her face faded to pink. Good. The ephedrine seemed to be working and allowing her to get oxygen to her lungs.

"Sure thing."

Patterson heard the man request an ambulance while he monitored the woman, who appeared to be in her late forties, probably a few years younger than his own fifty-four. Her eyes fluttered. "Ma'am?"

She drew in a ragged breath. "EpiPen?"

"I injected it in your leg."

"Thank you."

"An ambulance is on its way." He brushed a strand of hair off her forehead, feeling her still-flushed skin. He wished he had a bottle of water to give her but didn't want to leave her side to fetch one.

"Should be here in about ten minutes," said the man with the baby.

Patterson relayed the info to the woman in case she hadn't heard the man over the traffic whizzing by on Main Street, then checked on his niece and nephew. Both sat, legs swinging, on the bench by the library entrance.

Nola plucked at his sleeve. "Wasn't … accident."

"What?" He leaned closer. "What wasn't an accident?"

She blinked as if trying to bring him into focus. "Reaction."

He studied her but her steady gaze assured him she was cognizant of what she was saying. "Someone caused you to have an allergic reaction?"

She nodded, then her fingers grazed her backpack. "Coffee mug."

He glanced at her backpack, a turquoise insulated travel mug snug in the outside mesh pocket. He reached for it, but her words stopped him. "On it. Not in it."

Sirens screamed the arrival of the ambulance, which halted in one of the travel lanes closest to the sidewalk. The dog barked once and the woman laid a hand on the harness proclaiming it a therapy dog. "Molly."

"I'll take care of her." The kids would be delighted to spend a little time with the dog since they hadn't had a chance to during story time.

"Thank you." She closed her eyes as an EMT dashed up, kit in hand.

"What happened?" Even as he asked the question, the medical professional snapped on gloves and removed his stethoscope from the bag.

Patterson recounted what he'd done, pointing to the spent EpiPen lying beside the woman. He lingered there, his hand on the dog's harness.

"Hey there," the EMT said, touching the woman's shoulder. "Want to tell me your name?"

"Nola Johnson." The woman kept her eyes closed.

"What happened?" The EMT continued to monitor her while his partner unloaded the gurney from the ambulance.

"Allergic reaction." Nola drew in a shuddering breath. "Peanuts."

The EMT's partner arrived with the stretcher. "We need to get her loaded into the ambulance."

"I'll get out of your way." He picked up Nola's backpack and guided Molly over to where Hailey and Harrison waited. The children's delight at petting the dog brought a smile to his lips but his mind worried over the certainty in Nola's voice that someone had deliberately triggered a life-threatening allergic reaction in her.

Find out what happens to Nola and Patterson in Fatal Recall, *book two in Twin Oaks Secrets, coming summer of 2026.*

About Sarah Hamaker

Join Sarah's newsletter and receive one of her romantic suspense novellas for free! She shares about her writing journey and other Christian romantic suspense authors, plus subscribers get a chance to win a romantic suspense book each month! Join here: https://sarahhamakerfiction.ck.page

You can connect with Sarah on her website, sarahhamakerfiction.com, or on these social media platforms:

BookBub: https://www.bookbub.com/profile/sarah-hamaker

Facebook: https://www.facebook.com/authorsarahhamaker

Goodreads: https://www.goodreads.com/author/show/1804799.Sarah_Hamaker

Instagram: sarah.s.hamaker

LinkedIn: https://www.linkedin.com/in/sarah-hamaker-7295a01/

OTHER BOOKS BY SARAH HAMAKER

The Seeking Justice Series

Journalist Brogan Gilmore had been a rising star when an unethical shortcut on a story leads to his fall from grace. A chance encounter with convicted murderer Melender Harman a few months after her release from prison provides Brogan with a chance for career redemption—if he can land an interview with her.

After serving her 17-year sentence, Melender has one objective: To uncover the truth about what happened to her cousin the night the toddler disappeared. When Brogan pursues her for an exclusive story, she reluctantly agrees if he'll help her reexamine the original investigation into Jesse's presumed kidnapping and murder.

While re-investigating the case, Brogan struggles to keep his objectivity as he begins to believe Melender's innocent of the crime —and starts to envision a possible future together. Then a shocking discovery throws their relationship—and investigation—into turmoil.

As Brogan and Melender come closer to solving what happened to Jesse, will their budding relationship survive the truth?

Justice Denied

Jetta Ainsley's life had been complicated enough as she navigates cleaning out the family home while her mother recovers from a car accident. When her dog is hurt, her next-door neighbor Seth Whitman offers his help. Seth would like to do more for Jetta but the walls she's placed around her heart are unsurmountable.

Then she learns her late father had been accused of embezzlement, drawing Jetta into a web of secrets that could prove his innocence— or destroy her. When digging into her father's past brings danger to their doorstep, Jetta turns to Seth for assistance in uncovering who stole millions before someone gets hurt.

Seth tries to protect Jetta and her mother from the increasing danger, while clues lead them ever deeper into a tangled conspiracy. Unraveling the sinister plot will require all their courage, faith, and trust in each other.

But will uncovering the truth clear her father's name—or destroy their growing love for one another?

The Cold War Legacy Trilogy

Compelling stories about ordinary women uncovering extraordinary secrets of the past that could cost them everything.

The Cold War Legacy Book One: The Dark Guest

The Cold War is over, but The Wolf is still at the door.

"Once I started reading *The Dark Guest,* I could not put it down. The story captures the reader in the first chapter and doesn't let go until the last. Sarah Hamaker has created wonderful characters to root for as she takes them on a dangerous, twisty journey to the truth."

—Patricia Bradley

Author of The Natchez Trace Park Rangers Series

When Violet Lundy isn't cleaning rooms at Happy Hills Assisted Living Facility, she loves spending her free time with resident Rainer Kopecek. Hearing his stories of the dangerous life he led behind the Iron Curtain in East Berlin makes her own life seem more tolerable. But when Rainer is found dead and his room in disarray, Violet suspects foul play.

Dr. Henry Silverton lives among his books, teaching and writing about the Cold War. A letter about an East German traitor known only as "The Wolf" propels Henry out of academia and into Violet's life. Together, they embark on a perilous quest to uncover the truth about Rainer's death and the traitor's identity.

Can Violet and Henry uncover the secrets of the past before one of them ends up as The Wolf's next victim?

The Cold War Legacy Book Two: The Dark Atonement

A translator and a medical researcher team up to find a long-lost scientist with an innovative cancer treatment.

German translator Lena Hoffman thought her grandfather died years ago. But the unexpected arrival of a cryptic postcard seems to indicate otherwise. As Lena delves into her grandfather's past and uncovers information about him and his cancer research work in East Germany four decades ago, she unwittingly puts her own life in danger.

Dr. Devlin Mills works as a cancer researcher at the National Institutes of Health and lives across the hall from Lena, although they've never formally met. But when Lena is nearly run down by a vehicle, Devlin finds himself thrust into the role of protector. As their lives intersect, the pair find themselves in a race to discover the whereabouts of her grandfather—and whoever wants to silence him—before the past catches up with the present.

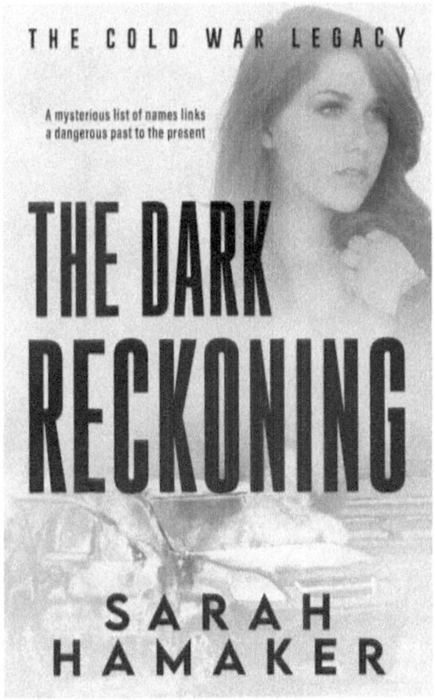

The Cold War Legacy Book Three: The Dark Reckoning

A mysterious list of names links a dangerous past to the present.

When Isana Thomas finds a smartphone among the cherry trees, her life is put in jeopardy. Isana discovers the phone belongs to Lillian

Hillam, whose son, Cyrus "Cy" Hillam, works at The Heritage Museum with Isana. But Lillian is missing, and someone doesn't want the pair to find her.

Cy can't believe his mother would disappear without telling him, not after his father's suicide when he was a child. Then kidnappers claiming to have Lillian contact him, asking to exchange her life for a list of names. Cy and Isana must delve deep into his parents' past to find the list and save his mother's life.

But someone doesn't want them to succeed and will do anything to stop their search. Will Cy and Isana uncover the truth about the list before their lives are snuffed out?

Love Inspired Suspense

Dangerous Christmas Memories

A witness in jeopardy…and a killer on the loose.

Hiding in witness protection is the only option for Priscilla

Anderson after witnessing a murder. Then Lucas Langsdale shows up claiming to be her husband right when a hit man finds her. With partial amnesia, she has no memory of her marriage or the killer's identity. Yet she will have to put her faith in Luc if they both want to live to see another day.

Vanished Without a Trace

A missing person case. A new clue. And a fight for survival.

After nine years searching for his missing sister, attorney Henderson Parker uncovers a clue that leads him to Twin Oaks, Virginia—and podcaster Elle Updike investigating the case. Partnering with the journalist is the last thing Henderson wants, until mysterious thugs make multiple attacks on both their lives. Now they'll have to trust each other...before the suspected kidnappers make them disappear for good.

Standalone Romantic Suspense

Illusion of Love (Seshva Press)

A suspicious online romance reconnects an agoraphobe and an old friend.

Psychiatrist Jared Quinby's investigation for the FBI leads him to his childhood friend, Mary Divers. Agoraphobic Mary has found love with online beau David. When David reveals his intention of becoming a missionary, Mary takes a leap of faith and accepts David's marriage proposal.

When Jared's case intersects with Mary's online relationship, she refuses to believe anything's amiss with David. When tragedy strikes, Mary pushes Jared away.

Will Jared convince Mary of the truth—and of his love for her—before it's too late?

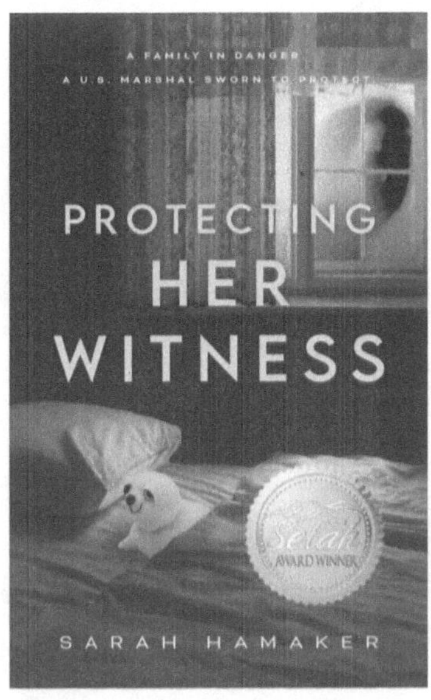

Protecting Her Witness (Seshva Press)

A family in danger…a U.S. Marshal sworn to protect.

U.S. Marshal Chalissa Manning has been running from her past and God for most of her life. When she meets widower Titus Davis and his son, Sam, her well-built defenses begin to crumble. But someone is targeting Titus and Sam, and it's up to Chalissa to both protect them and to find out who is behind the attacks.

As the threats pile up, will Chalissa be able to keep the family she's grown to love safe?

Novellas

Deadly Diamonds (Seshva Press)

The race to find missing diamonds puts a widow in danger.

Three years ago, Dulce Honeycutt's life imploded when her husband died after a robbing a jewelry store and her 18-year-old son, Kieran, landed in prison as an accessory. The uncut diamonds were never recovered, and when rumors fly that she and Kieran know where the gems are hidden, their lives are in danger.

Veteran insurance investigator Miles Sharp believes Dulce knows more about the diamonds than she's revealing. But as the attacks on the beautiful widow's life multiply, he struggles to maintain his professional objectivity. Is Dulce a victim or is her story a sweet web of lies?

Mistletoe & Murder (Seshva Press)

Alec Stratman comes home to Twin Oaks, Virginia, after his Army retirement to contemplate his reentry into civilian life. Instead he's greeted with the murder of his beloved Great-Aunt Heloise.

For Isabella Montoya, the loss of Heloise Stratman Thatcher goes beyond the end of a job. Heloise had encouraged Isabella to follow her dreams and helped fund her studies. Now, accused of her mentor's murder, Isabella is scrambling to prove her innocence.

Since his great-aunt had written glowing letters about Isabella, Alec is unwilling to believe the police's suspicion of the former housekeeper. Instead, he works to help clear her name.

Will Isabella and Alec be able to navigate the secrets that threaten to derail their budding romance and uncover the truth about Heloise's death before the killer strikes again?

Christmas Cold Case (Seshva Press)

All she wants for Christmas is to solve her parents' murders—and stay alive.

Noelle Chastain has returned to Twin Oaks to discover who killed her parents thirty years ago. When the Shenandoah County Sheriff's Office declines to reopen the cold case, citing lack of new evidence, attorney David Keener steps in to help her search—and keep her safe from someone who doesn't want her digging up the past.

Will they find out who's behind the increasingly personal attacks on Noelle before she suffers the same fate as her parents?

www.ingramcontent.com/pod-product-compliance
Lightning Source LLC
Chambersburg PA
CBHW032219190726
48289CB00007BA/2308